The Rustle of Leaves

The Rustle of Leaves

Nat Burns

Desert Palm Press

The Rustle of Leaves

by Nat Burns

© 2017 Nat Burns

ISBN (book): 9781942976547
ISBN (epub): 9781942976554
ISBN (pdf): 9781942976561

For permission requests, write to the publisher at lee@desertpalmpress.com or "Attention: Permissions Coordinator" at

Desert Palm Press
1961 Main Street, Suite 220
Watsonville, California 95076
www.desertpalmpress.com

Editor: CK King
Cover Design: Michele Bordeur - eebooWORX

Printed in the United States of America
First Edition October 2017

Acknowledgements

Thank you, my dearest Seeker (CK King) for making the editing process so pleasurable and for actually liking the book.

Many thanks to DPP publisher Lee, who approached me at a conference and said, 'write a horror book for me!' Her desire for horror brought me back to my days of writing eerie stories and science fiction only. Not a bad place, at all.

I need to especially thank my beloved Chris who, though abhorring the genre, read this draft many times through. Religiously. *Te amo*

.

Dedication

This book is dedicated to those amazing writers who have inspired my lifelong love of horror. The creepy, slowly unfolding tales of authors such as John Saul, Ira Levin, Anne Rice, Stephen King, and Shirley Jackson have entertained and deliciously terrified me into becoming a writer myself.

Chapter One

THE FUNERAL SEEMED TO drag on forever. Fortunately, it was filled with an unusual amount of lightheartedness. After all, old man Detter, whose mama had named him Ronald, was more than seventy-eight years old at his passing. He'd lived a good, long life. Everyone said so.

The pastor in the pulpit, Reverend Daniel Blevinth, was at his glorious best, extolling the virtues of one of God's most beloved children. Mary, one of the younger Detter daughters, who sat in the front pew, sniffed loudly and occasionally nodded her head in agreement with the kind words said about her father.

Bertie Madison, taking the afternoon off from her teaching job at Ryan Nash Elementary, shifted on the hard pew and crossed her arms across her lean belly. She was remembering the oldest Detter daughter's many bruises noted before the girl had, at age fifteen, run off with Cleet Preston and made a new home over in Crenshaw County. Bertie pressed her tongue against her top teeth and surreptitiously glanced at her watch. Surely this pomp and circumstance had to end soon. She was undecided whether she'd make the short trek to the gravesite. She owed the dead a huge measure of respect, but she was having a bad day and simply wasn't in the mood.

A smothered cough drew her attention. Sloane Stevens straightened in the seat next to her and quickly waved Bertie's pending concern away. Sloane, queer as a three-dollar bill, was dressed in her usual dyke wear—a baggy, dark-blue shirt and black leggings above heavy, black boots. Her short, ebony bangs were gelled into a formidable spikiness, and Bertie had an almost irresistible urge to reach over and smash them down.

A figure moved at the back of the church, catching her eye, and suddenly Bertie had a hard time lowering her gaze. Sheriff Lacey Terry, in her crisp blue uniform, stood near the door, watching the service from the back of the sanctuary. Damn, but she was a handsome woman. Though small in stature, she had presence, usually noticed right away whenever she entered a room. Maybe it was caused by her good posture, or maybe it was the perfect twist of long, black hair she wore pinned professionally to the back of her head. The style encouraged her stark cheekbones to protrude and brought attention to the odd brilliance of her blue eyes. Those eyes were like fine blue topaz, and when she laughed or smiled—a common occurrence—deep wrinkles framed those eyes, softening their intrinsic coldness with merriment.

Bertie turned her gaze back to the pulpit, even as her heart leapt in her chest and her breathing quickened. She pondered the reaction—fear or lust? She sighed. Only time would tell. Reverend Blevinth hit a new round of forcefulness, and several of those gathered jumped nervously as if awakening from a light sleep.

"Therefore, we sorrowfully give back to heaven our beloved friend, Ronald Detter, as we move onward and find our own peace in his passing, as he would wish us to do. Let us bow our heads in prayer."

Bertie surreptitiously studied the room during the prayer and found the small gathering was made up of the older people of the county, those who invariably, from an outdated notion of respect, came to just about every funeral. With a niggle of horror, Bertie wondered if she had become one of them. She only came to certain funerals, and she was still one of the younger ones, not yet forty. She glanced sideways at Sloane, wondering why she had come. Then she remembered that Sloane had gone to school with the youngest Detter daughter, LeAnn. Odd that Mary had come and LeAnn had not. Leticia Preston, the oldest, was also missing. Obviously, she had little respect for her father. Or maybe the two-hour drive had just been too much on a busy mom with kids too young for school.

"We will now continue this service at the gravesite," the reverend continued. "We hope that all of you will follow us. The processional will gather out in front of the church, and we ask that you keep your vehicle lights on until we get to the cemetery."

Bertie stood and stretched her lower back, still trying to decide if she would go to the cemetery. It wasn't like it was any great trek, being only a few rural blocks away.

"Hey, Bertie." The mellow voice sounded right next to her. She would know it anywhere.

"Hey, Lacey. How's the sheriff biz these days?"

Lacey laughed and the afternoon sunlight caught on her gold-plated badge, momentarily blinding Bertie. "Sheriff biz. Now, that's a new one on me. It's going well. You know I kept Wade's staff, so that's been a big help."

"Wade sure was a sore loser, wasn't he?" Bertie

asked with a short laugh.

"Well, not so as you'd see. He *tries* to keep it hidden."

Both women turned as one to glance at the portly ex-sheriff who was shaking hands and slapping backs.

"Cronies," Bertie said with a derisive sniff.

"Yep, sure right about that. Are you going to the cemetery? I get all creeped out seeing that big pile of dirt just waiting to be dumped on the coffin."

"Yeah, and what's even creepier is that they try to cover it with fake grass. Like this...this green blanket hiding the dirt so no one will see it there."

Both women shuddered.

"Maybe I'll just head on home," Bertie said, her mind finally made up.

"Wish I could. I have to go back to work for a spell. Then it'll be home with a pizza and a beer. Put my feet up." Lacey grinned and tugged on her belt.

"That sounds good. So, who's on call? Sully?"

Lacey nodded. "That would be him, our very own Deputy Sullivan Oates."

"Now, who in their right mind would name their child Sullivan?" Bertie asked testily.

"Oh, come on, you can't tell me you haven't seen worse names in ten years of teaching." Lacey's eyes sparked with merriment.

Bertie reflected. "I guess that's true. I have a real hard time with the kids whose moms were really creative. You know, names like Shaniqua spelled two ways. Or Devi-Shineonandon."

"I think you're making those names up," Lacey teased.

"Well, maybe, but you get what I'm saying."

"I do, I do," Lacey said. She pulled Bertie close in a

sideways hug. "Okay, back to work. You have a good afternoon, hear?"

Bertie, all aflutter from the other woman's touch, couldn't speak. She only waved as Lacey turned away.

Chapter Two

NANCY AMELIE, PUSHING EIGHTY years of age, moved with the strength and energy of a teenager. This eternal youthfulness often amazed her granddaughter, Lacey.

"I can't even get up from a chair without groaning," Lacey muttered into her tea mug.

"What's that you say?" Nancy asked absently. She was involved in deadheading the late fall roses blooming against the rough wood siding of the porch.

"How do you stay so young, Nanna? I feel old already, and I'm only thirty-two."

Nancy laughed and resumed her seat. She looked around the garden encroaching on the porch and nodded as if satisfied with the rampant growth surrounding them. A light breeze moved through, and the plants sagely nodded their heavy-flowered heads in response.

Nancy lifted her cup of tea and took a hefty swallow. "Age is only a state of mind. It's about how you think."

Lacey watched her with amusement. "So...I think I'm old and that makes it so?"

Nancy leaned forward and studied her granddaughter, her short white hair glistening in the slanting afternoon sunlight. "You're not old. You're just not paying attention. You need to find something that makes you feel...young."

Lacey heard the slight pause and understood the gentle rebuke. Yes, she needed to fall in love. She needed to engage more in life. She frowned. Like that could happen in tiny Queens Lot, Alabama, a population of just over nine hundred souls. She knew most of those nine hundred souls, had grown up with them. She knew their good traits and their failings. There was nothing like working on a police force to help you really get to know the people you shared a town with. It also helped you learn, very quickly, which ones should be avoided.

Lacey leaned forward and snared one of the tiny triangle sandwiches made of cream cheese and cucumber that her grandmother habitually included with afternoon tea. "So, back to you. What keeps you young?" She bit into the sandwich, and the rich sweetness made her jaws ache. "Mmm, you sprinkle sugar on these, don't you?

Nancy chuckled. "Sure. And that's the secret of youth. Sugar." After a short silence, she responded again. "I don't know, Lace. I just enjoy life. My life. I wake eagerly each morning and look forward to each day."

"So, it's as simple as that? I mean, I look forward to my days too...I guess." Lacey frowned and pondered about her job. It wasn't as bad as some, and she was heartily glad she wasn't a police officer in a big city.

"I hope the roses don't dry out too badly this winter," Nancy mused. "You do have a busy job though. A tough one at that. I'm not sure I'd look forward to doing what you do."

Lacey nodded and brushed crumbs from her hands onto the bright yellow, plastic tablecloth. Her maternal grandmother had always adored yellow, and it was included anywhere it could be included and still remain within the boundaries of good taste. "It's not too bad. The worst is the paperwork and dealing with the politics. That really gets on my nerves."

"Who's giving you grief?" Nancy cocked her head to one side, her gaze curious.

"Oh, you know. It's just part of the job. I work with great people. I thank God every day for Erva. I'd be lost without her."

"Speaking of Erva, I ran into her when I was leaving King's and she told me you went to Ronald's funeral. How was it? I just couldn't bring myself to face those girls. Thank goodness their mama passed when she did."

"It was okay." Lacey shrugged. "The usual funeral goers were there but no LeAnn or Leticia, just Mary. I think Norma's passing might have been a bad thing for the girls. You know, no one to run interference."

Nancy frowned and her fingers drummed the table in agitation. "As if she could have done anything. He ran that house with an iron fist. I still think he let her die by not taking her to the hospital. Surgery could have saved that woman."

"I know." Lacey sighed loudly. "I pushed Wade as hard as I could on that investigation. He was having none of it."

Nancy stirred restlessly and stood. "Useless piece of flesh. He was a horrible sheriff and is a hopeless human." She softened her tone when Lacey shook her head. "I know. I know. I don't mean to speak ill of your old boss, but you know it's true."

Lacey sighed and rose to stand next to her grandmother. She would never forget the supercilious bitterness in Wade Helms's face when she—a damn woman, for God's sake—won after running against him in the election. He had covered it quickly, but not before his chief deputy noticed. "And he's still an ass, talking smack all over Queens Lot, saying it was a rigged election. Crazy."

Nancy abruptly grabbed Lacey's hand. "Enough about him. Come and see. I finished the new painting!"

Lacey laughed aloud as she lurched off the porch and was pulled along by her grandmother. "Whoa! Slow down. I may not be off the clock, but you don't have to hurry."

Nancy released her hand and laughed sheepishly. "I just get so excited about finishing a new piece."

"I know. I'm surprised you didn't lead off with that when I got here. Guess it's because I found you working in the garden."

Her grandmother moved forward at a more sedate pace.

"Did it turn out the way you wanted?" Lacey asked a moment later.

Nancy paused and turned to face Lacey. "Well, of course! I just keep pounding away at it until it's exactly right."

"Pounding?" Lacey raised one eyebrow and her grandmother haughtily frowned at her before turning away.

Nancy's studio was off the kitchen side of the house. It was semi-attached to the main house, fixed by one wall to the overlarge kitchen. Lacey guessed that the room had once been the original kitchen because of a bricked in doorway in the attached wall and the huge fireplace on one of the outer walls. This fireplace was now covered completely by her grandmother's older paintings, making an improvised gallery. The rest of the room was mostly unfurnished except for a ratty floral sofa and an end table against one windowed wall, and the cushioned stool and wooden easel in the center of a large paint-spattered rug that covered the rough wooden floor. A long, narrow table on another wall held her painting supplies.

"Oh, Nanna! It's magnificent," Lacey said on a heavy release of breath.

Nancy's style was considered abstract, because she had developed a unique technique of simply following the paint. It began with heavy acrylic paint, one layer, with colors chosen impulsively. When this had completely dried, a layer of water was applied and then watercolors poured gingerly across the slanted surface. Then her grandmother would use brushes to portray the hidden figures her mind perceived residing within the two layers. After another full drying, another layer of watercolor was applied judiciously, to bring out the imagined images created by the earlier layers.

This huge painting, brewing under her creative hands for a full twelve weeks, had blurred into a magnificent, but subtle, Pegasus-like horse in smooth shades of purple and green. One graphite-gray hoof touched gently into a rushing white and cobalt river, and neon-silver lightning bolts flashed across an expanse of sapphire sky. The many layered, almost three-dimensional wings hovered against the muscled body with bright snowy highlights on each feather.

"So, you like it," Nancy commented quietly, one thumbnail pressed to her bottom lip. She was critically eyeing the painting, as she stood studying it alongside Lacey.

"Oh, yes, I do!" Lacey exclaimed. "And it's so big! It really draws you into the scene."

Nancy sighed. "I sensed that it needed to be big. Just a hunch, really, but it worked out well, I think."

Lacey laughed and put a hand over her mouth. "Duh!"

Nancy's happiness seemed to rebound and fill the studio. "Should I make it the centerpiece?"

"In the show? Of course! You'd be crazy not to."

Her grandmother was guaranteed an annual show in downtown Mobile every winter, and the usually successful sales gave her grandmother a good bit of extra income for the year.

"It keeps me young, I guess," Nancy said slowly, grinning at her granddaughter.

"Aww, Nanna, you are just so…so perfect!"

Lacey drew her grandmother into a prolonged hug, rocking their bodies from side to side as they laughed together.

Chapter Three

""YOU KNOW, IF YOU was just a little bit pretty, maybe you wouldn't be caught up lookin' after me," Mol Allison said, as her daughter Debra slowly rubbed lotion on her varicosed and bruised-looking legs. "You could have some kind of useless life all your own."

"I'm pretty enough," Debra replied tiredly, automatically, as she carefully rubbed the lotion into her mother's gnarled skin.

Mol chewed an imaginary cud and rested a disdainful gaze on Debra. "You so fulla shit. I just can't get over who fills you' head with this trash."

Debra reared back and wiped the lotion from her hands with a ratty old cloth. She tossed it to one side, onto a small pile of Mol's discarded debris, and then rose to her full height. She looked down at Mol, hatred rebounding through her like a tennis ball trapped against the net. "Well, people at the schools. People who got some sense! I look after you because it's my duty, not because I'm ugly like you say."

Mol flipped her faded housedress across her exposed knees and leaned forward on her cane. "You don' owe me nothin'. Just 'cause I borned you and wiped your ass all them years."

Debra lit a cigarette with shaking hands and took a seat in the dog chewed easy chair. She stared at her mother through the smoky haze, thinking how much better the old hag looked when shaded that way. Mol had gone to overeating and overdrinking, neither habit doing her aging body much good. Today, her hair was still uncombed and greasy, clumped strands hanging limply on either side of her deeply lined, pasty face.

"What the fuck are you lookin' at?" Mol said sharply.

Debra looked away, her gaze falling on the window. It was so dirty and pockmarked that she couldn't see anything outside, but the diminished light was welcome.

"You better look thataway! Shame, I say. It's damned hard to get any respect these days. When I was workin' for Shell Oil, I got yes ma'ams and no ma'ams from everyone I saw. Now, you come over here lordin' it over me like you somebody." Mol chewed on her false teeth furiously, and they made that clicking sound that always annoyed Debra.

"I am somebody," Debra replied sullenly.

"Oh, all 'cause you got a big-time job with the grocery? Glorified checkout girl, is all." Mol lifted her glass and drained it. "Here, be a waitress. Pro'lly would pay more. Get me some whiskey, damn it!" She shook the glass at her daughter.

Debra crushed out her cigarette and rose, snatching the glass from Mol. "I manage the goddamned place, and you know that as well as you know your own name."

She moved quickly into the kitchen, setting her mother's two stinky mutts, Duff and Daisy, to barking, even as Mol muttered more slights behind her. She slowed and leaned one hip against the counter. After placing the glass next to the half-empty bottle of bourbon beside the cracked, dish-filled, ceramic sink, she scrubbed at her face with both hands.

God, she hated living with this bitch. She'd never had a father, just a string of her mother's boyfriends who sometimes liked Debra just a little more than her uncouth parent. Debra had never fought or called them names when they molested her. If only her mother had kept her damned mouth shut more often, maybe those men would have been satisfied with her and not sought out Debra.

Both Debra's siblings had escaped early on, leaving Debra to deal with the aging behemoth in the other room. Then they'd died. Her older brother, Donnie, died on a motorcycle on a cold, icy road in Virginia; and her younger sister, Ellie, overdosed on street heroin in Louisiana.

Them leaving her to deal with their mother had been all right. Debra felt no ill will toward them. Them dying had been okay, too. She'd expected it. What sat hard with her was the way her mother had reacted each time she was told that a child of hers had died. There was no remorse, no sadness, just a cold, blunt edge of sarcasm. That bothered Debra in a huge way.

"Stupid bitch," she muttered as she poured Mol a new drink. Taking a deep breath, she strode back into the cluttered front room and held out the glass.

Mol eagerly took a long swallow before placing it on the table next to her chair and lighting a cigarette. She air-swiped Debra aside and pressed the mute button on the remote. Loud voices filled the room, and Debra recognized them immediately. Posturing city cops investigating heinous murders. Her mother was obsessed with police procedural shows, and she'd watch the same ones over and over at every opportunity. At one point, Debra herself even had the shows memorized. Not anymore. She had other interests.

Debra sighed and slowly strode down the hall to her bedroom. She closed the door quietly, gratefully. Yes, she was often lonely, but that loneliness was a blessed relief after listening to Mol ramble on with her negative prattle. Debra glanced around her small room. She kept it neat, to counteract her mother's slovenliness, but the room was crammed full. Fold-up tables served as desks, each bearing computer components. She had two desktop computers with their large towers, as well as six laptops, each plugged in to its own multipurpose dock. Several Android tablets peppered the tabletops, and her two smart phones were charging in their cradles.

This was her home. Here, she could be better. Here, she could step into the real world of her avatars, the alternate personalities she wanted to be. She could talk to men, men who wanted her, men who thought her beautiful.

Her hand trailed across the specially built computer that she used to hack into bank accounts and even the freakin' Federal Bureau of God Almighty Investigation. Yes, she could go anywhere and do anything with the touch of a finger.

"Take that, Mol, you old snake," she whispered.

Her mother knew nothing about computers, and that fact had spurred Debra's interest. It felt good to have this one thing that Mol hadn't put her negative touch upon. Without her mother's knowledge, Debra had taken a few courses in computer science at the community college and then several online courses in computer engineering. She was delighted to discover that she seemed to have a natural affinity for the machines. They responded well to her.

The larger towers and monitors had been brought in during Mol's infrequent trips out of the house. She had no idea what was in this room. She never would. Debra turned back and engaged the four deadbolts. She slid into the center chair, one finger brightening the oversized screen. She had a little work to do. She opened the local bank's website and logged into the password buster she habitually used. The old man may have been computer illiterate, and he may not have set up an online access account. But, then again, his daughters might have done it for him for his auto deposits.

It was usually a race against time when she did this. As soon as the relatives started nosing around, they would see the money and her work would be noticed. Getting in right away, during the hours after putting the loved one to rest, was imperative. The computer beeped quietly, and she pressed two buttons to gain access. Surprisingly, he didn't have much, only seven thousand. She wouldn't take it all. She usually left at least a thousand, just so the heirs wouldn't be too put out. Carefully, slowly, in fifty-dollar increments, she moved most of the money into the dummy account. Each time money was transferred, she scrubbed all traces of the transaction. All traces. Each time. And she did it again, just to be sure. When only a little over a thousand remained in the old man's account and traces of the past few monthly deposits had been removed, Debra sat back and folded her hands over her ample belly. Just let Social Security try that on for size. Another successful robbery.

The Benevolent Mother would be pleased.

Chapter Four

MOTHER KNEW THE PLACE very well. Called Three Pigs for its fabulous pulled pork sandwiches, the bar was located on the southern outskirts of Queens Lot, far out into rural Coves County. These types of places always were on the outskirts and, lucky for her, people who disappeared from such places were seldom missed for very long. And she so needed a specific new boy, a pretty-faced angel.

The heat and humidity was brutal on this night, and she wondered idly what the hell she was doing staying in this part of the country. She should have settled up north somewhere. Maybe it was true, what people often said, that habit really was stronger than hate.

One would think that an occasional cool breeze would meander through from the scenic Tombigbee River. Mother, sitting outside studying the Three Pigs middle-of-the-night clientele, felt no such relief.

Finally, a perfect boy sauntered toward the entrance to the bar, and Mother pushed her damp bangs from her forehead. He was pretty—cropped hair a faultless bottle blond, designer jeans tight enough to hug and emphasize his package, his AC/DC black T-shirt tight across his ripped abdomen. *Umhmm.* His bright eyes scanned the parking lot and lit briefly on Mother sitting in the shadows. His gaze passed away from her dismissively, as he pulled open the glass door.

Mother took in a deep breath. "And so it begins," she muttered.

Hitching up her jeans, she moved toward the entrance of the bar. It was comfortingly dim inside. Lame music sounded from a cheesy, glowing jukebox, and an older couple danced with surprising skill on the small, wooden dance floor. Mother watched them a moment—making sure she didn't know them—before sliding onto one of the barstools.

"Hey, nice lady. What'll it be?" the older, weathered bartender asked, as he leaned on the bar in front of her. Mother flashed him one of her practiced Kewpie-doll smiles.

"Vodka and Co-cola."

He grinned at her and turned away, as she fished a ten out of her pocket and laid it on the pitted bar surface. She pinned it down with a bowl of unshelled peanuts.

"Here you go, doll." The bartender expertly placed the napkin and highball glass in front of her. He slid out the ten. "You just let me know when you need anything else," he said slowly.

Mother ignored him and sipped the cold drink, as she stared at her reflection in the large mirror at the back of the bar. Even distorted by the rail bottles, she looked good. Her long wig, as well as her choice of youthful clothing, fooled many into thinking she under thirty. Odd that, since she wasn't exactly the best at healthy living.

Her eyes strayed to one side, searching for the boy who'd entered ahead of her. She finally spied him in a back corner, his blond, spiky hair gleaming in the lounge spotlights, as he gestured energetically with his friends.

Mother's eyes narrowed. Were they *really* his friends? If so, she might have to reconsider. Her plan did not include friends and the young boy being missed by them. She preferred to acquire the disenfranchised, those who were on the fringes of polite society. Those easy to transform into her angels.

Then she saw it—the subtle proposition as Blond Boy morphed into seductive mode. His target responded as one would expect, the smile widening and attitude becoming more eager. The blond's younger companions looked knowingly at one another, then rose and wandered toward the pool tables.

Target and Blond Boy moved closer together. They were laughing and snickering with few words. Blond Boy touched Target's leg under the table, a move clearly visible from Mother's vantage point.

Mother liked gay men, loved to experience their blinding passion vicariously. It—this passion— consumed them until they acted carelessly. It made them blind to everything around them, and Mother had used that to her advantage many times during the past few decades.

Blond Boy rose and took the target's hand, pulling him toward the lavatories. A strange spike of arousal moved through Mother. She could imagine, in detail, what they would do in those porcelain-throned stalls. Would Blond Boy suck the target off, jerk him off? Would Blond Boy offer his sweet, narrow bum?

Mother lifted her drink and took a healthy swallow. Less than twenty minutes later, Blond Boy reappeared. His flirtatious smile was gone, and he just looked pinched, tired. His eyes searched the room, no doubt looking for another target. Or maybe just a friend.

Maybe a mother.

"So, was he good?" Mother asked as Blond Boy passed near the bar.

His eyes narrowed as he studied her. He paused, uncertainly. "Do I know you? You look familiar but...what would you know about it?" He scowled. "You a cop?"

Mother laughed and shook her head. "Not hardly. I just want to buy you a drink. You look like someone I'd like to get to know."

He eyed her with rampant speculation. "Salty dog," he barked to the bartender, his eyes never wavering from Mother. He addressed her quietly. "Just know that I'm not into girls. I can try if you wanna, but it's just not my thing."

"I know," Mother said in tacit agreement. She placed a twenty on the bar, knowing it would keep the barkeep quiet, and the two of them moved to a booth in the back. Mother sat in the shadows, not wanting Blond Boy to catch too good a glimpse of her face. Yet.

"So, how was he?" she asked again, once they were settled.

"What the fuck do you care?" he asked. He took a healthy swig of his drink.

She shrugged. "I'm a voyeur. I like to imagine."

He cocked an eyebrow even as he scowled at her. "Seriously? How pervie."

She leaned forward and crossed her arms on the tabletop. "I'm wondering what you really think of these johns."

Watching her like she had three heads, Blond Boy shifted in his seat. "It's just a job," he said finally. "I get the old fucks off, and they pay my rent. I don't think about them much at all."

"So, if they weren't here…?"

"Hell, I'd starve and be homeless," he exclaimed.

"What if you could have a new, rent-free home and as much money as you wanted?" She watched his eyes closely. As expected, they lit slightly and widened.

"I think that's a real fine pipe dream." He pulverized a small cube of ice between his perfect teeth.

"I can make that happen," she said quietly, as she leaned back. "Just say the word."

His gaze fell to Mother's hands and she clasped them together on the tabletop. "Just what do I have to do to get all this wonderful stuff?"

She shrugged. "Just what you're doing now."

He chuckled and drained his drink. "I don't need no pimp. I got all the action I can handle on my own and there ain't no extra, if you get my drift."

"Oh, I do. I do, and that's okay, perfectly all right." She drained her own glass, the ice clinking loudly as she placed it on the table.

He watched her in amazement, and then laughed again. "You're a piece of work, ain't you? Comin' up in here like this, sayin' these things."

Mother laughed with him. "Yeah, well, I'm done talking. I'm heading out. It's late."

"You mean early. It's almost daylight. I got a late start here tonight."

"Tell you what, since I took some of your time, lemme give you a little something." Mother fished in the change pocket of her jeans and brought out a folded fifty. "Here, take this."

He took it without hesitation, but his manner became seductive. "Sure I can't do somethin' for you, you bein' so generous and all?"

She studied his youthful face and smiled slowly. "Well, you could walk me to my car, if you would. I get scared at night, going out there by myself."

He, as she knew he would, assumed she wanted more and grinned widely as he got to his feet. He held out a bent elbow, and rising, she took it with a girlish giggle.

Outside the air-conditioned bar, the air was still thick and muggy. Mother found it hard to get in a deep breath. A saving grace was the light scents of bald cypress and elm wafting through on the heated, early morning air.

"I'm back here," Mother said, leading Blond Boy around to the back of the bar. It was darker here and no one would see Danny's car. She took Blond Boy's hand, and they giggled again as if this were a great adventure. She led him to the car, her free hand pulling the patch from her pocket.

"Come on over here and show me what you've got, pretty boy," she cooed in a whisper. She leaned her back against Danny's old Chevrolet and pulled Blond Boy close. She pressed herself against him.

"Hey, let's try this," she said, waving the foil wrapped packet toward him.

He paused doubtfully in his approach. "I dunno. I just do a little weed. I don't like the hard stuff."

Mother grinned and, after stuffing the packet back into her pocket, pulled a thin blunt from her bra. Blond Boy eagerly fished a lighter from his pocket and offered it. Mother lifted it to her lips. "Pure gold. From Mexico way."

"Mmm, the good stuff," he mused, moving close.

"Here, I'm being rude. You first." She placed the blunt between his lips. She glanced around then lit him up. Smoke erupted and he sucked it in eagerly. "Tasty," he said, holding his breath.

"Oh, I know," Mother said, caressing him along both sides of his waist. "Enjoy it, baby, and we'll fly right on out of here."

He laughed out a great cloud of smoke and hit the blunt again. The red, glowing eye at the end of the cigarette was beautiful in the dusky, fading darkness.

Danny stepped from the car just as Blond Boy's eyes rolled back in his head and he crumpled soundlessly to the ground.

"Get his head," Mother ordered quietly as she shifted around to lift his long legs. Danny grinned at her in the darkness and crawled through the back seat, drawing Blond Boy in head first. Mother bent Blond Boy's legs and tucked them into the car. She leaned and fetched the burned blunt from the ground, looking around for signs of their presence.

"I'll drive. You ride back there with him." She scrambled into the driver's seat, her eyes scanning the surrounding area to make sure they weren't seen.

"He's pretty," Danny said from the back seat. She glanced back and saw that he was caressing Blond Boy's cheeks and smoothing his T-shirt.

"Yes, he is, isn't he?" she replied, shifting the car into gear.

Chapter Five

THE COVES COUNTY SHERIFF'S Department was quiet, unusual for a Friday afternoon, but Lacey was damned glad. She'd had a busy week catching up on paperwork and closing a few investigations, and she was ready for a break.

"Some wedding," she muttered as she shuffled a small stack of papers.

Alicee Sherman had married Roy Bennett two weeks ago but, before they could get a solid start on their nuptial journey, someone had decided to split both of them stem to stern with a hunting knife. In their bed. Lacey shuddered, even now bothered by the random violence. Especially so since all leads seemed to have washed out and they were no closer to finding the perpetrator.

Queens Lot was a quaint, small town and had very little viciousness such as this. Most of Lacey's staff dealt with minor traffic infractions, deadbeat dads, and the drunk and disorderly. There was a fight now and then, leading to charges of assault. But often, after a make-up beer in Portia's Pub or the Three Pigs, charges were dropped with much good will. Every now and then there was an accidental death, from a car accident or other mishap, but this purposeful knifing, this brutal, deliberate murder—well, it just didn't fit into the paradigm of Queens Lot.

Defeated, she placed the file in the cold case basket for Erva to file then rose and brewed a single-serve pod of dark coffee. She scrubbed at her face as she waited, and then ruefully added a good bit of chemical-laced creamer to the cup. Sipping the hot brew cautiously, she resumed her seat.

"Coffee time already?" Erva Williams asked as she moved quickly into the room. "Must be workin' on paperwork."

Lacey grunted. "You know it."

"Okay if Frank lets Carson go home?" Erva asked.

"Frank's still here? I figured he'd gone home long ago." Sergeant Frank Wright, the county jailer, wasn't known for long hours but then, he wasn't a young man either.

"He was doing the same thing you are, pushin' the paper." Erva sat in one of the office chairs on the other side of Lacey's desk and watched her. Lacey finally lifted her gaze.

"What?" she asked, scowling.

"Can Carson get out of the drunk tank?" Erva asked, as she mimed impatiently.

Lacey nodded and waved her assent and began tidying up the folders on her desk.

Erva remained, unmoving.

"What?" Lacey asked with a deep sigh.

"What are you doin' this weekend?" Erva asked finally, tilting her round head to one side.

Lacey studied Erva's sweet, grandmotherly face. She wasn't even truly middle-aged yet, but she had always mothered everyone she'd ever met. She was a good manager, too, smoothly transitioning staff and office from one sheriff to another after the election.

"Why do you want to know?"

"Wanna come over for dinner? Mister is barbecuing." She watched Lacey coyly.

"All right. Who are you trying to hook me up with now?" Lacey leaned back in her chair and laughed.

Erva laughed as well. "Naw, it ain't like that—this time. Your mama and daddy are coming. Thought you might like to, too."

"Cook me a veggie burger?" Lacey squinted at her receptionist.

"Of course. And the beer will be ice cold." Erva grinned. "Now, if you want me to invite some hot, young man, you just say the word."

Lacey barked a loud negative response. "There's no way I could deal with my parents *and* some slue-footed man you brung around."

Erva stood and laid several folders on Lacey's desk. "Sunday at two, after church, and here's some folders from Judge Serge. He says you have to go in and testify on that reckless driving charge."

"Oh man! Why did I have to stop that crazy guy? He's been nothing but a pain in my ass since." She lifted the folders and cracked them, glancing at the summons. "Says here he swerved 'cause there was a cow in the road. I didn't see no frickin' cow, and I was right behind him."

"Daylight, too," Erva agreed with a slight hum. She moved toward the door then turned back. "Don't you think it was weird the way Ronnie Detter died?"

Lacey looked up. "What? Just old age, I thought."

Erva grunted in response.

"Why? What did you hear?" Erva and her husband, Lloyd, were great resources for community information that might not otherwise make it to the ears of the law.

"Jimmy said that the neighbors, you know, the Hales, Axel? Well, he told Jimmy that some man had been hanging around a week or so before Ronnie died."

Lacey hadn't heard this. "When did he tell Jimmy?"

Erva shrugged. "I don't know for sure. I think it was just in passin', you know, guy talk." She waved one hand dismissively.

"Hmm," Lacey grew thoughtful, the Sherman-Bennett murder foremost in her mind. "Thanks, Erva. I'll look into it. I'm sure it's nothing."

"Yeah, no harm in checkin' on it." Erva nodded decisively and finally ambled from the room.

Lacey sat deep in thought. Seems a lot of the Queens Lot older citizens had been passing away lately. She sat a moment or two longer before standing. Anything to get away from paperwork.

She found Jimmy in the breakroom. Oddly, he wasn't doing anything, just sitting at the lunch table, staring at the wall.

"Oh, good," she said, taking a seat across from him. "You're still here."

Jimmy grinned and shrugged. "Ain't in no hurry."

Lacey thought Reverend Jimmy Ross and his late wife, Shirley, had once been the handsomest couple in Queens Lot. They were charismatic, too, as evidenced by their huge congregation at the Pentecostal church. Some said Shirley had been preparing to host a morning religious program on a local, predominately African-American radio station. Then had come her sudden death due to a bad heart that no one knew she had. Everything changed. Jimmy stepped down from the pulpit at the Rising Soul Free Will Church and come to work as chaplain for outgoing Sheriff Helms. He seemed to be handling the enormous changes wrought in his life with great aplomb, but it was no surprise he wasn't rushing off to go home.

"Listen, I was talking to Erva and she said you'd heard something about Ronnie's death. That true?"

He scrubbed blunt fingers through his short, grizzled hair. "Well, I was talking to Axel after the funeral, and he was saying that some man had been hanging around but he hadn't seen him at any of the family nights. Seemed odd to him."

"So, the guy just disappeared? What did he look like?" Lacey crossed her ankles and leaned her forearms on the table, curiosity lighting her features.

"Well, I kinda felt him out about that, but he wasn't too forthcoming. Said his girl, Alexa, watched him more, liked the way he looked and all." Jimmy frowned apologetically.

"Okay. Maybe I'll mosey on out there tomorrow and have a talk with her."

Jimmy nodded. "Yep, yep," he muttered.

"So. Do you think there's anything suspicious about Ronnie's passing? I mean he was way on up there in age."

Jimmy shook his head as if perplexed. "Now, I don't rightly know. Seventy-some ain't so old. You thinkin' about ordering him dug up and examined?"

"Oh, gosh no. You watch too much TV," she chuckled fondly. "At that age, though, it's unlikely that he was murdered. What would be the motive?"

"Money? Revenge?" Jimmy tugged at the round white collar he wore under the folded collar of his dark-blue uniform.

Lacey shook her head pensively. "Unlikely. If anything, it was some kind of accident, some tussle."

"And you're thinking he got hurt. Maybe was too

old to recover?" Jimmy blinked slowly.

"Maybe. But we need to find out who he was with before he died. Do you know where the body was in the home? I wasn't able to make it out there 'til after he was brought to Clevon's."

"I think they found him in the kitchen. He was on the floor."

"That could mean anything. Or nothing," Lacey mused, forefinger pressed to her chin. "I guess I'll take the file home and read it tonight."

"Good idea," he agreed, rising. "Speaking of home, I guess I'll be off mysel'."

Lacey studied him. "You okay, Chaplain? You doing all right?"

"One day at a time, Miss Lacey. One day at a time," he said, shaking his head as though it weighed a good bit.

Lacey rose too and lightly rubbed Jimmy's back. "That's the only way, Jimmy. But if you need anything, you just let me know, okay? We're all here for you."

Jimmy smiled tremulously. "Thank you, Lacey. You know I appreciate everything y'all do for me."

Lacey watched him leave the breakroom, his back bowed with loss. She felt oddly helpless.

Chapter Six

THE TOWN OF QUEEN'S Lot was gearing up for Halloween, since the holiday was a little more than a week away. Every store on Hawthorne Street offered ghoulish decorations in each glass fronted display. Lacey remembered the keen fear she'd felt, as a little girl, upon first seeing the bandage-wrapped figure sitting in a chair on Lockhart Preston's lawn. The mummy had jumped up and come after her and her parents, white bandages trailing. If Lacey hadn't gone to the bathroom just before leaving home, she had no doubt she would have wet herself. Big time.

It had been a long while, probably on into high school, before she truly understood the fun others imparted into the day. Now as an adult and sheriff of a small town, she wasn't looking forward to the thirty-first. Halloween always meant a lot of extra work for the sheriff's department and its bare-bones staff.

Lacey drove the white Coves County police cruiser slowly along Hawthorne. Even on Saturday, the streets were sparsely populated. It was early though, just nigh onto nine, so it was no surprise. Just about everyone liked to sleep in on the weekends. Lacey would have liked to, as well, but she'd had a hard time sleeping. Perhaps reading about Ronnie Detter's death may have been the reason. There were a few things she'd read that troubled her.

One, Ronnie had received a glowing health report on his physical just a few weeks ago. The complete exam had included a scan that would have picked up any ballooning aneurisms or artery plugs. Clevon Stringer, county coroner and mortician at the Forever Rest Funeral Home, had sent in for Ronnie's medical records from town doctor, Beasley Moore, and included them in the file copies he'd given the department. Probably because, as he'd stated, there was no overt cause of death. He had listed the cause of death as unconfirmed, likely a fatal heart attack or arrhythmia.

Secondly, Ronnie was not alone when he succumbed to whatever killed him. Two of his daughters had been there at the house, visiting. Could they have somehow banded together and killed him? They certainly had reason enough, if the rumors were true. That would be a sticky wicket, arresting and prosecuting those girls who had already suffered so much abuse.

Thirdly, Clevon had jotted a short note in his records about two things—abnormally small pupils, even well into death, and an unusual limpness to the muscles of the body. He hadn't offered any reasons, of course, but that note raised red flags in Lacey's mind.

She sighed and shifted in her seat. Maybe she should go talk to Bertie on Monday. She'd taught two of the three girls at Ryan Nash Elementary. It wouldn't hurt to get to the bottom of Ronnie's character, at the very least. If the girls *had* done something, Lacey would deal with the fallout later.

At Al's Pump and Save, Hawthorne bore left, toward Highway-17 that would take her up to Choctaw County, but Lacey bore right onto a secondary road that led past the Detter property. Ronald Detter had inherited a small hay farm from his father, Enid. It had been a good producer, even supplying nutrition for Kentucky thoroughbreds, and it was no surprise because of all the hard work that went into the place.

Ronnie took his inheritance seriously. Woe unto anyone who didn't take the work or the farming lifestyle just as seriously. Unfortunately, Ronnie's wife, Norma, had borne only daughters, and his bitterness seemed to have grown with each birth. Perhaps, he thought females couldn't love and maintain the property as well as sons would have.

"And look at him, just as dead, regardless," Lacey muttered with some bitterness of her own.

The Detter hayfields had gone all golden now, and Lacey idly wondered if there would be one last harvest before the mild, southwestern Alabama winter set in. Driving past the large, white farmhouse set less than a quarter mile off the road, Lacey pulled in to the house next door. Due to some weird property lines, the neighbor's place sat catty-corner to the Detter house. She stepped from the cruiser and turned to study the Detter home, frowning at the black wreath on the door. Visibility was good. It was conceivable that Alexa Hales could have seen anyone entering or leaving the house. She turned and looked at the Hales house, wondering which window was Alexa's room.

"Well, hello there, Sheriff. What in the world brings you out here on this cool Saturday mornin'?" Bonnie Hales walked toward her across the lawn, wiping her hands on a blue gingham dish towel. She paused in front of Lacey expectantly.

"Good morning, Bonnie. I hope it's not too early for a house call?"

Bonnie grimaced in dismissal. "Of course not. You know you're always welcome here. Come on inside. I just put on a new pot of coffee, and we'll have us a nice visit."

Lacey followed Bonnie inside, her mind absently marveling at how well Bonnie's jeans fit in the bottom. She had a nice figure, and the scuttlebutt was she was flirting a bit with Moe Mosser over at the Circuit Ride Gym. Maybe that's why she was looking so fit and trim.

Inside, Lacey picked up the scents of bacon and biscuits and knew the family had enjoyed a hearty breakfast. She followed Bonnie into the kitchen and found her two teen children, Adam and Alexa, standing at the dishwasher. They both looked up when the two women entered the room.

"Hey, Sheriff," Adam said genially.

"Hey there, Adam."

"Get the sheriff a cup of coffee, Alexa," Bonnie said, pulling a chair out from under the table and indicating that Lacey should sit. Lacey complied and seconds later, she was staring into the depths of a mug of black coffee.

"Here's some cream and sugar." Alexa quietly indicated the items she had just placed on the table.

"You need anything else, Mama?" Adam asked Bonnie, as he hovered near the doorway.

"No, go on." Bonnie waved him away, as she took a seat across from Lacey and prepared her own mug of coffee. "Be sure and tell me, if you go off to the mall, you hear?"

"Yeah, sure," he said absently as he left the room. Obviously, the boy didn't have a lick of curiosity about why Lacey was visiting.

Alexa was different. She slid onto a chair next to

Lacey and cupped her chin in one palm, waiting expectantly.

"So, what can we do for you, Lacey? Is your visit business, or are you just being social?"

Lacey chuckled. "A little of both, actually. I hear that some stranger, a man, was hanging out over at Ronnie's place. Did either of you see him, talk to him?"

"Well, I didn't see him." Bonnie blew on her coffee. "Alexa did come ask me about him one day, askin' if I knew who he was."

"So, you saw him?" Lacey turned her attention to Alexa. "Had you ever seen him before?"

The girl shifted her position, sitting up straighter in her chair. She snared a long lock of her straight, cherry-wood-colored hair and twirled it around a forefinger. "No, never. He was just real handsome. Skinny though, almost too skinny. Like he hadn't grown into hisself yet."

"What color was his hair? How tall was he?" Lacey leaned forward.

As if intimidated, Alexa leaned away and dropped her hands. "Well, he was dark-haired...about the same height as my daddy, I guess."

"Just under six feet," Bonnie added helpfully.

"And have you seen him since?" Lacey asked Alexa.

"No, I haven't and I been lookin' for him. I saw him off and on last week, maybe three days. He seemed real friendly with Mister Detter. They was laughing and shaking hands and all."

Lacey grunted quietly. "I know this seems a little like overkill, but do you think you could come with me over to Frances's house and see if she could draw us up a sketch of this man?"

Alexa frowned. "I guess so. Do you think he did

somethin' to Mister Detter? I mean, he didn't look mean or nothing. Just a normal looking guy…come to think of it though, he was missin' one of his front teeth. You know, people, especially young people, just don't let that happen anymore. They go on over to Doc Halpern and get on his payment plan."

Lacey pressed a forefinger to her bottom lip. "Sounds like maybe he wasn't a local. You have no idea what business he had with Ronnie?"

"Most of the men who come for the hayin' are dressed like field hands, you know," Bonnie interjected.

"Or they have suits, like tryin' to sell him something." Alexa added. "This guy, he was young and dressed in just an old T-shirt and jeans. Worn-out athletic shoes."

Silence fell as they mulled this information.

"Well, let's get a drawing and see where we can go from there," Lacey said finally.

"I'll get my jacket," Alexa said as she left the kitchen.

"I sure hope no one did anything to Ronnie. We first figured he died in his sleep…and then later on we thought he'd had a heart attack or something," Bonnie said worriedly.

"His girls were there that day, weren't they?"

"Yes, but only the two youngest. They were there and left early. Well, one did. Mary left about midday to get something, dinner she said. When she came back, he was acting strange when they ate, kinda wobbly, she said. Then he just lay down on the sofa and fell dead. I was out trimming back the marigolds, and I never have heard such shrieking."

"Did you go over?"

Bonnie nodded. "I did, felt for his pulse and

everything. Alexa called the fire house."

"Did Mary say anything else?"

"Just that he was really sleepy while they were eating but that she thought he was okay." Bonnie shrugged. "She was fussing at him about leaving the back door open, and he fell plumb asleep."

Lacey saw that Alexa had returned so she stood. "Sleepy? That's kinda strange."

"That's what Mary said when we went over. You know, after her daddy died," Alexa said.

"I've told the sheriff all that," Bonnie said chidingly. She rose and the trio walked to the door.

"Behave yourself and don't give Sheriff Terry any trouble now," Bonnie said to her daughter, as she straightened the girl's light jacket. "Will you have her long, Sheriff? I told Grandmother Bowling we'd be over later today."

"Oh no, an hour or so is all," Lacey answered. "Frances is a fast sketch artist."

Chapter Seven

"SO, SCHOOL IS GOOD?" Lacey asked once the two of them were settled in the car and heading toward town.

"Oh, sure," Alexa responded, shifting in her seat. Her perfume filled the cruiser with the scent of some kind of sweet fruit…maybe strawberry? "I just wish Mama would ease up on the dating rule. Says I've got be seventeen before I can even go on a group date. How crazy is that? All my friends get to go out together, but Mama and Daddy still say no every time I ask."

Lacey nodded her head in solidarity. "She's just worried about your safety is all."

Alexa chuffed. "As if! What bad thing happens in little ol' Queens Lot? It's about as safe as being at home in your very own bed."

Lacey shook her head. "I wouldn't say that, Alexa. There's crazies everywhere. People out to do evil for evil's sake. Believe me, it can happen."

"Have you ever seen anything really bad happen? You know, bein' Sheriff and all?" She watched Lacey curiously. "I heard about the newlyweds who were murdered."

Lacey frowned. "Yes, but that's rare here. We don't have a lot of crime but I do see police blotters from other towns all around us and you just don't want to take a chance on it. Really."

She pulled the car into Frances's drive, switched off the engine, and turned to Alexa. "Tell you what you do. We have this woman who comes around from time to time and teaches self-defense down at the station. I'll let you know next time she comes in. Should be in a couple weeks or maybe next month. Take her class and then, when you can show your parents that you can responsibly defend yourself, maybe they'll let you group date, at least."

Alexa opened the car door and Lacey followed. "You know, that is a good idea. I can be a bad ass." Alexa struck a pose and mimed an attack.

"Umhmm," Lacey commented, as she knocked on Frances's door.

Frances Corey was as eccentric as they come. She had moved to Queens Lot more than a decade ago and made a tidy living teaching art to the local housewives. She also sold her paintings at area craft shows. Once she was voted in as Sheriff, Lacey had decided that, since there was no position in place for a police sketch artist, she would use Frances as an impromptu solution. She paid her twenty dollars a sketch, out of her own pocket, and the two previous times she had used her, the sketches had been invaluable.

"Hey, Sheriff," Frances said, as she opened the door. "Come in, come in. Excuse the mess. You know how messy we artists are."

Alexa's eyes grew wide as she took in the male nude on the canvas in the center of the living room slash studio. Lacey grinned, wondering whether Alexa was more shocked by the nude or by the art debris littering every square inch of the room.

"Come on back here, and I'll get us some iced tea," Frances said.

They followed her into a bright, large kitchen, almost as cluttered but certainly more manageable. Lacey took a seat at the table and beckoned Alexa to another chair. Alexa slipped off her jacket and hung it on the ladder back of the chair. Frances brought three glasses to the table, as Lacey shifted some small canvases to the side.

"Yes, yes, move anything you need to. I just get so busy," she explained weakly.

"Do you think you'd have a little time to do a sketch for us?" Lacey asked.

"Well, of course. Be happy to. Let me get the tea."

Lacey studied Frances as she turned away. Today, Frances was in jeans and a T-shirt covered by a dried-paint-smeared, khaki-colored vest. Several paintbrushes protruded from one of the vest pockets and two art pencils stuck out, points down, from another one. Lacey wondered, yet again, how Frances did anything with her waist-length, graying hair swaying around her all the time.

Frances cleared a space and placed a cold pitcher of tea on the table. "Let me get my sketch pad," she said, scurrying from the room.

Alexa looked at Lacey and shrugged with a tolerant expression. She leaned to pour tea in her glass. She tasted it. "Yum, sweet tea."

Lacey poured hers, as Frances re-entered the room.

"Here we go." Frances set about clearing space on the table, placing piles of prints and unopened mail on the fourth chair at the table. She laid out her sketch pad and smoothed the blank page with her palm. "I assume we're sketching something you saw, young miss?" Frances said pleasantly, as she took a seat and helped herself to tea.

"Yes, ma'am. It's a man," Alexa responded politely.

Frances answered Lacey's unspoken question by pulling her hair from behind her back and, after twisting it, expertly pinning it up with a skinny paintbrush she fetched from one pocket. "Well, then, let's talk about his head. Was it more round or more oval, like an egg?"

"Like an egg," Alexa responded. "But like, flat, or square, on the bottom."

Frances nodded as her hands, as if disconnected from her body, swept over the page, the pencil in her hand making light marks on the sketchbook page. "So, it was like this then? Square?"

"Umhmm. But with a little point in the middle. You know, like a pointy chin. He was really skinny too, like a little kid, though he was full growed."

"And his ears? Were they low down on his head or high up? Or in the middle, maybe?"

"I'd say middle," Alexa said thoughtfully. "And they stuck out a little bit. He had long hair, to his shoulders almost, and you could still see the ears, like peeping through."

Frances nodded. "Ahh. So he's a white man, I'm guessing? Was it like this maybe?" She tilted the notebook on the table toward Alexa.

Lacey saw the faintest outline, but Alexa responded eagerly.

"Yeah! Yeah, like that. Yes, he was a white man."

Frances took a long pull on her tea. "Was there anything else you noticed about his face. You know, that was different or stuck out? Maybe something you don't see every day?"

"Well, he was missing one of his front teeth, which is kinda weird."

"Ummhmm," Frances agreed. "What did his mouth look like. Big lips, little lips? Did he have a big smile?"

Alexa thought about it. "It was a nice smile. Friendly."

Frances took out a short ruler from yet another pocket and used it to measure the face. "Okay. I'll just use regular lips. What about his eyes? Were they together? Far apart? What color were they?"

"Gosh, that's tough. See, I saw him from far away, like across the road, and I couldn't really see his eyes. I remember thinking how good looking he was, if that's any help."

Frances had drawn a faint cross in the center of the man's face and was expertly forming eyes and a mouth.

"Sure, sure. Every little bit helps. Now, about his nose. Was it pointy? Flat? Little? Big? Did it fit his face?" Frances watched Alexa closely as she pondered the questions.

Alexa wriggled in her chair and trapped a hand under each thigh. She was thinking hard. "Pointy. Like sharp even," she said finally. "It wasn't too big, but I remember it was a little pointy."

"You're doing really well," Lacey said encouragingly, as she smoothed the girl's back with one palm.

Alexa smiled at her and a silence fell, as Frances magically shaded the sketch.

"I wish I could paint," Alexa said eventually. Her voice was a reverent whisper.

"Can you draw at all?" Lacey asked, just as quietly.

"Some. I like to draw horses. I have this one in my room. I'll show it to you next time you come over."

"It's got to be a passion," Frances interjected. "Something you have to do every day, no matter what.

When I was a kid, I never went anywhere without a little sketchpad or even a lined notebook. I just drew and drew and drew." She turned the notebook around so they could see the drawing. "Is this him?"

Lacey studied the nonchalant portrait. It was a young man, somewhat hippie-like in appearance. Frances had portrayed him smiling and, indeed, it was an engaging smile, even rakish, given the missing front incisor. His hair was long and straight, parted in the middle, which made his nose appear even pointier than Frances had no doubt intended. She had drawn his shoulders narrow, probably to indicate his slimness, and she had given him a standard T-shirt neckline.

"Omigosh," Alexa breathed. "That's him! That's him exactly!"

Chapter Eight

"I DO SO LIKE the blueberry tarts," Corey Tallmayer said with a hum of pleasure. He took another bite, and then grinned sheepishly. "But I guess you can tell that from my boyish figure...or lack thereof."

"Nonsense, sweet boy. It does me a world of good to have someone to tend to again." Maureen Arrington leaned back in her floral-patterned, cushioned chair.

They were on the back verandah, as usual. The one that overlooked the back garden. The porch had an overhang, so they weren't troubled by the afternoon sun. Plus, the vista was breathtaking. It encompassed the wide, peaceful Tombigbee River and green-swathed mountains just beyond.

Even the yard was magnificent. Maureen had won honors from the Queen's Garden, the local horticultural society, and her hollyhocks *were* amazing. Corey could pick out roses, brown-eyed Susans, azaleas, lots of rust and yellow chrysanthemums, and orange and yellow daylilies all around. And these were only the ones he recognized. Maureen had so many, it was mind boggling, and she had a lot of decorative grasses, which really helped border the garden in imaginative ways.

"Well, you just tend away, Miss Maureen. You know I won't be complainin.'" Corey rested his hands on his plump thighs and visually examined one of the large gold rings he habitually wore. He noted that his new, expensive watch was already getting tight. He made a mental note to go up into Chatom, to the mall jewelry store, and get another link for the band.

"When my sweet Tommy married that jezebel and moved all the way to Birmingham, I was fit to be tied. Not even gonna be any grandchildren either, with both of them so wrapped up in their fancy careers," she said mournfully. "I just figured I'd spent the rest of my days as an old, unwanted woman."

Corey looked at her so that she would think he was listening intently. In actuality, he'd heard it all before and many times. Being alone with her, which was the way it had to be, meant that there were no other people or any distractions to change her mournful tune. Tommy had been the one and only child of Maureen and her late husband, Quincy, and mother and son had once been very close. Maureen was having a lot of trouble with the separation, especially as she lived alone and probably found herself at loose ends more often than not. Truthfully, she was a lot more socially connected than he had anticipated.

She turned a bright smile on Corey. "So, as I was saying, having you to take care of suits me just fine. Wasn't it clever how we found one another?"

Corey laughed and ran his hand over his carefully buzz-cut hair. "I guess friends don't often meet over a slab of pork loin and find out they have so much in common so quickly. Such as arguing about how it should be cooked."

"I know. But you have to admit. That pork loin was just fine eatin' after I got done with it. I daresay better than you would have done." She simpered girlishly even though her eightieth year had come and gone.

Corey lifted his cup, remembering to extend his pinky, and took a sip of the now tepid brew. His mother had insisted on afternoon tea, as well, and Corey had abided by that training for all of his twenty-four years even though, personally, he didn't see the attraction. He guessed it was the social interaction, because a full English afternoon tea always meant conversation—especially gossip—and lots of it.

"Sad about Ronnie Detter, wasn't it?" Maureen said, lifting her own teacup.

An unexpected breeze came through, and Corey felt suddenly chilled. He sat his cup down. "Yes. I was so upset. I personally didn't know the man well, just seeing him at the shop-and-go, you know, but he seemed like a nice enough fellow."

"Well, there's some that say the world's a better place being shed of him. And some that just might have wanted to help him on his way." She nodded emphatically and the loose flesh on her face shook.

Corey leaned forward avidly. "No! You don't think someone would commit murder right here in Queens Lot, do you?"

Maureen looked away imperiously. "Stranger things have happened, you know. I understand he just wasn't good to his family, nor his workers, and that's all I'm saying about that."

"Well, I'll be," Corey exclaimed. "I never would have thought that in a million years." He plucked a lemon-poppy mini-muffin from the tray of offerings and fingered it between his thumb and forefinger. "Still, don't you think it could have been natural causes? He wasn't a spring chicken, you know.

Maureen laughed and leaned back in her chair again, teacup contents sloshing dangerously close to the rim. "Neither am I, my dear, neither am I."

They fell into a companionable silence again. Maureen leaned forward and chose a small tart which she popped into her mouth. Corey watched her chew.

"So, are they sure that the cancer is in remission?" he asked.

She shrugged and swallowed. "That's what they tell me. Not that it can't come back. There's a five-year window, and if it's not back in five years, I'll be cancer free. Ain't that a blip? I may not even live to see that. A woman my age is just glad she wakes up in the morning."

Corey grunted in answer. He stood clumsily and began stacking the dishes. "I'm gonna clear up, and then you and me should mosey on inside. It's getting cool out here."

"It is coming up onto that time of year. I need to order up some candy. Believe it or not, we have a few tricksters that come out beggin' for candy each year...even way out here."

"And I bet you spoil them rotten," he said teasingly, as he held the door for her. "You probably even drop half dollars in their bags with the candy, don't you?"

Maureen paused. "Now, isn't that a good idea?" She started moving forward again, her cane tapping on the polished wooden floor of the dining room. "It'll have to be full-on dollars though."

"Why?" He sat the dishes in the sink and began to run water on them. "Because the half dollars are no longer in circulation?"

She pushed past him to bag up the remaining tarts and muffins. "Not really, more to do with inflation. A young un today would turn his nose up at half a dollar."

"Hell, you might even get grief if you give them only *one* dollar," he joked then laughed. Sudsy water ready, he turned the faucet off. "Sit down right there, little ma'am. I'm gonna go get the last."

Outside, he whistled lightly as he stacked dishes and cups onto a tray. He lifted Maureen's cup and gently rubbed, with the pad of his thumb, where her red lipstick had stained the rim. Placing it on the table, he poured in a little tea from the cozy-covered teapot. He glanced toward the house then slowly snared a vial from his trouser pocket. He tipped three drops into the cup then, replacing the vial, placed the cup on the tray. A rustle sounded behind him, and he saw that two angels had gathered to see Maureen off. He smiled and nodded at them, and the two angels took one another's hands. His heart thrilled at their whispered chanting. Whistling anew, he went back into the house, carrying the tray.

Chapter Nine

LACEY'S POLICE RADIO SQUAWKED to life Sunday morning, waking her from a comfortable sleep. She rolled over and checked her cell phone. Yep, the ringer was off. Now, how did she do that? She grabbed for the radio only to have her fingers glance off it and spin it from the nightstand and onto the floor.

"Hell and damnation!" she swore as she rolled her legs off the side and sat unsteadily on the bed. Her long, dark-chestnut hair fell forward and covered her eyes. She plucked the radio from the floor before sweeping the mane away from her face.

"Lacey here. What's going on? Over," she said into the radio.

"We been tryin' to get you for the past twenty minutes, boss. Is your phone broke? Over."

She could hear the humor in Sully's voice and smiled, even though she was still, technically, asleep. "Turned the damn ringer off, accidentally. Sorry. Over."

"Shore you wasn't...um...entertaining? Over." Sully chuckled.

"Not hardly! Open radio, Sully," she gently reprimanded him. "What's goin' on? Over."

"We got another death. Missus Maureen Arrington. She died at home. Over."

"Oh, no." She took in a deep breath. She

remembered Mrs. Arrington very well. She and her grandmother were gardening buddies. "Who found her? Over."

The radio squawked loudly then calmed as Sully's voice came through. "Housekeeper, Jenny Rodriguez. She was comin' over early to set up for a luncheon today. Found her layin' on the sofa, dead as a doornail. Over."

"Has Clevon gotten there yet? Over."

"Yep. Just got here. Over.

"Tell him to wait for me. I'll be out there as soon as I get dressed. Over."

He signed off, and she rose slowly. Damn. Another elderly person dying. Things were starting to get a little strange in Queens Lot. Could this many deaths be normal?

She hurried into the bathroom and jumped into the shower. After a few seconds, a chill ran up her spine, even under the heat of the pounding water. Had there been a strange noise? She ceased all movement, listening intently to see if she could pinpoint what had caused such a subconscious, visceral reaction. She debated turning off the water but laughed at her irrational fear. She finished soaping up then rinsed her face and turned to rinse her back. Suddenly, an unfamiliar noise filled and echoed in the small room. A creaking noise. Alarmed, she slammed water from her face and saw, through squinted eyes, that the half-open door to the bathroom was moving. Quickly, heart pounding with alarm, she swiped water from her eyes once again and peered around the curtain.

The husky cry of her Siamese, Ben, relieved her and set her racing heart back to normal. Man, was she jumpy!

"Shit, Bennikin! You scared me half to death, sneakin' in here like that!"

Ben watched her with an inscrutable gaze. He curved his lean body against the porcelain of the toilet, never taking his bright, blue eyes off her.

"You got nothin'? Really?" She shook her head in exasperation, slammed the curtain shut and finished bathing.

He watched her dress. Impatiently.

"Yes, I know. You want your morning meat. Can I, at least, finish getting myself together?"

Ben meowed loudly in response. He seemed to be getting irate. It was almost as if he knew Sunday mornings were supposed to mean long, leisurely breakfasts in the kitchen. In pajamas. Instead, his mom was preparing to go to work, yet again. Almost as if it weren't the weekend.

Lacey sighed heavily, as she clipped the radio onto her belt. "I know, Ben, I know. I'll be back as soon as I can, okay?"

Ben headed down the hall toward the kitchen. He looked back once to make sure she had gotten the message. Later, while he was wolfing down his canned breakfast, Lacey paused to brew some coffee and pour it into an insulated travel mug. It was going to be a long morning.

Pulling up to Bloom Haven, the Arrington farm, Lacey took in the unusually calm police scene. The other Coves County Sheriff's Department vehicle, a white Ford SUV, was parked next to the dark-blue Forever Rest van. A small foreign-made sedan rounded out the trio. Lacey assumed that was the housekeeper's car, and that Maureen's Chevrolet Impala was in the garage.

She stepped from the cruiser and turned to the

house. House? It was almost a mansion. Quincy Arrington had owned the Chevrolet dealership in town, and he had done very well for himself and his small family. Maureen had never worked, as far as Lacey knew, but she had brought in a good bit of award money from biannual gardening contests. In her heyday, she had been quite the impressive community leader.

Sully came out onto the wide front verandah as Lacey approached the house.

"Hey, Sully. Good way to start the morning, isn't it?"

"There's worse ways, I guess." Sully turned and led the way into the huge entrance hall. "We could be her."

"True." Lacey nodded in agreement.

"Hey there, Lacey. Good morning." Clevon was kneeling next to the body but stood to greet her. Maureen's body was curled up on the sofa behind him. She looked peaceful.

"Natural causes?" Lacey asked.

Clevon, a small, wiry man who, during off hours, had a rampant, bawdy sense of humor, grinned at her. "I should think so, Lacey. I mean she was eighty-two and had been battling cancer for a while."

Lacey pulled at her bottom lip as she pondered this. "Listen, Clevon. We need to be real careful on this one. Call it a gut feeling, if you want, but I need you to compare her death with some of the others that have been happening here in the Lot."

Clevon watched her, puzzlement twisting his lean face. "What? You think that these are homicides? That's a stretch, Lacey. Who would want to target old people? Old people. They get sick, they die."

She shrugged, bristling a little. She always had to

push so flipping hard at this job, especially when it came to dealing with the men. "Maybe no one is. Let's just make sure we keep our eyes peeled about everything from here on out."

Clevon scowled and turned away. "Whatever."

He spoke to his young helper who waited with the stretcher. "Let's get her out of here, Bobby. Looks like we'll be spending a good part of the day with her."

Chapter Ten

IT WAS ABOUT QUARTER after two by the time Lacey arrived at Erva and Lloyd's house, located at the southern end of town. She parked her cruiser next to her parents' sedan but remained in the car. She was still a little bit spooked, unusual for her. The interview with Jenny, Maureen's housekeeper, had been emotionally draining. Jenny had really liked Maureen, as employer and friend, and Jenny had been there, helping out and giving moral support during the two bouts of chemotherapy that had put Maureen's cancer in remission. To find her dead so suddenly had been extremely hard on her. Tears and emotional outbursts had delayed the interview and had choked Lacey up as well.

Later, touring the house for evidence, Lacey had noted the remains of a high afternoon tea but everything used had been washed and placed in the dish rack to dry. Lacey noticed right away that there had been two cups used. This ran counter to Jenny's testimony that no one had been scheduled to come by for a visit on Saturday. A friendly, check-in phone call from Maureen to Jenny the afternoon before had made no mention of anyone coming to visit Bloom Haven.

Lacey had also noted that two chairs sat askew to the table set on the back verandah. Could be something or could be nothing. She nibbled at her bottom lip, wondering why this situation had her so on edge. It was a crazy idea to think that someone was going around murdering old people. They were usually pretty inoffensive and tended to band together in little elderly people pods. It was odd, actually, to believe that someone would want to infiltrate those pods and murder for no real reason. But maybe there was some weird motive she hadn't thought of as yet. Angrily, she pushed open the door and stepped from the car. The scent of mesquite barbecue assailed her right away.

She strode around to the back yard and there they were, her family and friends, strewn lazily all across Erva's back patio. Her beautiful mother, her handsome father, her amazing grandmother, as well as Lloyd, dressed in his usual nonwork attire—mismatched, checkered Bermuda shorts and wild, Hawaiian-style shirt.

"Well, look who decided to trail in," Erva said as she set a bowl of potato salad on the round, latticed patio table. The table was already groaning under more than a dozen other dishes.

"Yum!" Lacey exclaimed, taking in the feast with a slow glance. "Sorry I'm late. Had a death this morning."

"Oh no, who?" Lacey's mother asked, as she rose to embrace her in welcome.

Joy Terry was about as perfect as a mother could be. Especially in Lacey's eyes. Her children, two girls and a boy, had indisputably been her reason for living. Even now, with Louie married and living way off in Utah, Lacey on her own as the Queens Lot sheriff, and the youngest, Lainie, off to Virginia Tech, their mother had blossomed in her own right, teaching yoga at the southside campus of Coves County Community College.

You could tell, too. She was small in build but strong and flexible, having practiced yoga since she was a girl.

Lacey, who realized that she had to tell her grandmother the grim news, must have been staring, because Joy shook her gently by the shoulders. "Hello! Earth to Lacey. Lacey, come in."

Lacey shook her head, clearing it. "Sorry, Mom. Woolgathering."

"Well, who was it, Lace?" Her grandmother, who looked so much like an older version of her mother, had risen and moved close.

There was no help for it. Lacey turned to her and took both her hands and held them. "Oh, Nanna, I'm so sorry. It's Mrs. Arrington. Miss Maureen."

Nancy blinked twice, hard, as though she'd been physically hit. "But...what? I just talked to her yesterday morning and...."

Joy rushed to embrace her mother, gently easing her from Lacey's grasp. She pulled her aside, holding her close, then returned her to her chair and sat down next to her, comforting her.

"What happened?" Erva asked quietly, as she moved next to Lacey. "Did she have an accident?"

Lacey hugged herself, wrapping her arms around herself as far as possible. "It was natural causes, Clevon says. The housekeeper discovered her on the sofa this morning. Looked like she'd just fallen asleep."

"Poor Jenny," Erva said.

"Yeah, it was pretty hard on her. Maybe you could give her a call later this evening?"

Erva nodded then frowned in deep thought as she spoke slowly. "Lace, don't take this wrong, or maybe see it as weird. I don't know. I mean, I been keepin' track, and this is like the seventh or eighth 'natural cause' death lately..."

Lacey nodded grimly. "Yeah. I noticed that, too," she said, their heads close together. "What do you make of it?"

Erva widened her deep brown eyes and shrugged as she shook her head. "No clue, but...."

"What happened, honey?" Lacey's father, Nathan, asked as he moved close. He'd finished the intense conversation he'd been having with Lloyd.

"Maureen Arrington died last night. I guess in her sleep," Lacey responded, wrapping an arm around his back and giving him a quick squeeze in greeting. "Ah, hell," he muttered. "Excuse me, Lace."

He strode to Joy and Nancy and knelt, holding them both as they tried to come to grips with the news. His murmurs of comfort wafted to Lacey and Erva.

Lloyd approached with a platter of burgers and hot dogs, two lonely veggie burgers leaning off the edge. "Something happen, Erva?" He waited, searching both their faces expectantly. Sweat wound slowly down his full, mahogany cheeks.

Lacey explained yet again, and Lloyd carefully placed the platter on the table. "Somethin's not right about this, Sheriff. I feel like there's been a funeral once or twice a month lately, when usually we go to only two or maybe three a year. It shouldn't be this way." He took a bandana from his back pocket and mopped at his face.

"You know, now that I think about it, that's true." Nathan returned, overhearing the conversation. "I wonder what brought about such a change. That's pretty extreme."

Lacey nodded. "Yeah, I know, Dad. Just occurred to me the other day when someone said they'd seen a stranger at Ronnie's house the few days leading up to his death. Struck me as suspicious."

"A stranger? But surely you don't think someone is killing people," Lloyd interjected. "I mean, who would do that? I figured there was maybe some kind of toxic, environmental thing going on. Why would some stranger come in to Queens Lot and kill people?"

"And they're older folks, not young kids out for trouble. Or druggies. Not even the drinkers. These are solid people," Erva whispered loudly.

Lacey sighed heavily. "I have no idea. It may be nothing, maybe no real crimes happening, but I plan to get to the bottom of it."

"You do that, sweetheart. And let me know if I can do anything to help with your investigation," Nathan said.

Erva sighed and pulled the metal chairs farther from the table. "Come on everyone, we need to send Miss Maureen properly on her way. You know darn well that she wouldn't tolerate tears."

The Terry's, Lloyd and Nanna, slowly came to the table. After all, Erva and Lloyd had gone to such trouble, but it was a subdued bunch who finally found their way back to normal, pleasant conversation.

Chapter Eleven

THE LAWRENCE HOUSE, TWENTY-five miles south of Queens Lot, was big, certainly big enough for the family. Each angel could have his or her own room, whether they used it full-time or not. There was a narrow servant stairway on the back, north side of the house that let any of them come and go without bothering the others. Cars could be parked in the huge crumbling barns around back as well, even though no one would notice if they didn't. The house was about a mile from any surfaced road.

Built in eighteen eighty-nine, the wood-framed, clapboard house teemed with memories, ghosts of the many residents who had lived there in the past. Mother could sense them. But then, she'd always had the gift, even as a very young child. When she, as a child, had remarked that she could no longer see someone's face, everyone in her family, even though the faces appeared normal to them, knew that the person would soon have a date with death. The gift scared some of her family members, delighted others. Mother had always been a little ambivalent about it. It's just how things were in her life.

The spirits could speak to her, if she wanted to let her guard down that much. Though sympathetic to their vast sense of loss, she had found no joy in letting them communicate. She much preferred the angst of the living.

That's why the skinny, poverty-stricken child from the deep bayous of South Louisiana had left home as soon as she could. The fewer people who knew about her abilities, the better. If anyone was going to exploit that gift, it would be her and no one else.

Oh, at first she had relished the attention bestowed upon her by the crowds of people who gathered together when her father forced her to perform. She'd been the special, adored darling. At least until the crowds went away. Then she became the freak, the idiot child locked in the back room of a cramped trailer. She did this for years, watching with an ever more jaded eye, as her father pocketed all the earnings from his weird child's performances. When her mother objected, he beat her and even turned that anger on the older and younger siblings. Her baby sister, Reese, was born with the gift as well, but her mother and she never told Reese's secret. Neither of them wanted her to be exploited like her older sister.

It was Reese's eyes she saw most, out of all those who had left her. The six-year-old had known about the fire before it happened, before Mother lit the match, but she hadn't told a soul nor tried to escape. She had planted herself at the bedroom window and watched her older sister, one hand raised in farewell, until the fire wrapped her in its fiery arms. She never even cried out. Now, as the Benevolent Mother, that weird little girl lived a life of total secrecy, gaining power by gleaning occult knowledge from the world around her. And she liked it that way.

Mother stubbed out her cigarette and reclined on the sofa. She gazed at her beloved Benevolent Angels, situated around the living room. Her heart warmed, swelling with joy and affection. She had a nice family growing. This was a newly formed family, and she felt like, this time, she had truly become a better mother. She was able to help her angels become even more invisible than they had been on their own, thus safe from those who believed differently than they believed. She had also taught them the importance of living by her commandments, and they had taken to the teachings well.

The taking of the original family of Benevolent Angels had been horrific. It had been necessary, however, as the policemen were closing in. Mother was fourteen and working illegally at the nursing home. She took them gently, calling them into her workroom one at a time and smothering them slowly, calmly, a hand across their mouth and nose. Their gazes were direct and tender, their eyes never leaving Mother's loving face until they were gone. Afterward, she had arranged their bodies with exacting care, making sure they were beautiful in their death.

"Bathsheba, please pray more quietly," Mother murmured.

Bathsheba Righteous, with ebony skin and an unbelievably thin, wraithlike figure, had a high, shrill voice that could prove wearying after some hours of praying out loud.

The taking of her other dear families, during years past, had been much the same, although many had died at the hands of those in power. Died by bullets and without Mother's final blessing and send-off. Those excruciatingly painful passages still lingered like an untreated cavity, even these years later.

"Yes, Mother," Bathsheba said amiably, and her

chanting voice became almost inaudible. She continued to rock back and forth on her knees as she faced the corner of the room. From an easy chair nearby, Danny kept his usual spellbound watch over her.

Mother didn't understand the fascination he had with the older woman. Maybe he saw in her a maternal figure. His own mother, rest in peace, had also been a religious zealot. Maybe he admired that familiarity in Bathsheba. He would eventually turn away from her and watched television with the same avid gaze. He was an odd one, no doubt, but he was good at running under the often difficult, homed-in, small-town radar. He seemed like a harmless, homeless youth, a bothersome gnat, swatted away and easily ignored. Yet, he was a handsome little thing, with fine features and silky hair. Mother had offered to take him into the next county and have his tooth repaired, but he wasn't concerned with the mar. And best of all, his meth habit was largely dealt with. He knew, without preamble, that he could only use the drug manufactured by Sarah Angel and only within the confines of the Lawrence house. And then, only until it started to affect his appearance or actions. There would be no trespass.

Her eyes traveled to Debra, who was unusually troubled today. More than half of the substantial Arrington money had been transferred without a problem, so Mother wasn't sure what the issue was. She would have to listen with her mind.

Debra sat at the dining table, fingers flipping across the keyboard of a laptop. Mother frowned, wondering what the woman was so busy with. She had a portable router, one blinded to public access, but Mother could see the tiny light flashing, proving that Debra was indeed online.

"Thank you, Debra, for all you do for the family," she said, loud enough to be heard above the TV noise. "You do realize how much we appreciate you, don't you?"

Debra turned a preoccupied gaze on Mother. Once their eyes met, she smiled widely, as she had been programmed to do, and her eyes softened markedly.

"Yes, Mother, but it is kind of you to say so."

"Can I do anything for you, Angel? Do you need anything?" Mother's voice was soft and loving.

Debra smiled, her eyes still locked with Mother's. "No, thank you. I'm very happy."

Mother dropped her gaze, and Debra returned to her keyboard. Blond Boy, who she now knew was named Kenton Walsh, entered the room, still staggering from the breakdown session he'd had earlier. His changeover was almost complete, and Mother was happy with his progress.

"Come here, sweet angel," Mother said, opening her arms expectantly. "Let Mother comfort you."

Kenton looked toward her blankly, but when their eyes met, he smiled and loped across the room toward her. He was like a puppy that hadn't grown into his big paws yet. Mother smiled as he fell into her arms. He stuck his thumb in his mouth and drew his long legs onto the sofa next to her. She smoothed his short blond hair and rocked him gently.

"Aww, Mother," Corey said, as he entered the room. "So sweet." He sat close to Kenton and began to stroke his legs and feet gently, as the three watched television.

"It's almost time," Mother whispered loudly.

As if on cue, Sarah Felton entered the living room. She carried the sacred box and placed it reverently on the low, round coffee table in the center of the room.

"Thank you, Angel." Mother extended her free hand and touched Sarah's burn-disfigured left limb. Sarah grasped her with the two fingers that remained on her left hand, and they stared deeply into one another's eyes for more than a minute.

"My darlings, my Benevolent Angels," Mother began, slowly breaking the connection with Sarah. She righted Kenton so he was seated properly on the sofa, next to Corey before reaching to switch off the TV. "Tonight, we honor the passing of Maureen Arrington who has found the freedom of everlasting peace."

Sarah opened the box and began laying out ranks of small pillared candles. "Louisiana," she said quietly on the fourteenth candle. Another rank was laid in place. It held twenty-eight candles. "Texas," Sarah whispered. The next rank held twelve. "Arkansas." Twenty-one candles. "Mississippi." After the final rank of eight was laid, Sarah closed the lid on the box. "Alabama," she said as she began lighting all of them, beginning with Louisiana.

The rest of the family watched reverently as each candle flickered to life. "We honor these souls who no longer suffer pain, hunger, homelessness, or being forgotten because of their age. We allow them to be free of medication, of strife, of rejection. We, as no others do, dearly love each of the souls represented here today."

The seven of them knelt and joined hands around the low table. They swayed rhythmically from side to side, as Bathsheba lifted her high soprano voice in song. It was an old, old melody, one Mother had learned from her Creole grandmother. All in French, it was a slow zydeco song, and Mother was not sure she ever knew what the words meant, although she knew it had something to do with that good night that comes to all. The melodic French words seemed to swelled her heart with love and affection each time she heard or sang it, so she had taught the song to her very first angels and had continued the practice. Now, Bathsheba's soprano mixed well when Danny's tenor and Corey's bass joined in.

Tears dampened Mother's cheeks, as she sang the song with every bit of fervor in her being.

Chapter Twelve

"DO YOU THINK HE molested them, as well as beat on them?" Lacey asked quietly.

Bertie shifted her deep brown eyes and deliberated a long minute. Finally, she sighed. "I can't say. I have no evidence of that. I have seen the bruises, however, and I've seen abusive interaction between Ronnie and Letty, his oldest. They had a horrible argument outside the school one day."

"They wouldn't have had anything to do with his death, would they?" Lacey asked hopefully.

Bertie tutted and waved a hand. "No, I seriously doubt that." She thoughtfully sipped from her mug of beer.

Lacey always enjoyed coming to Bertie's home. It reminded her of her grandmother's house, warm and cozy with just a hint of disorder. Just so one knew that the owner wasn't perfect. Bertie was big into crocheting and piles of yarn scattered the living room, awaiting her ministrations. Her crocheted handiwork also dotted the room. Luxuriously hued blankets rested on the back of two easy chairs and on the long brocade sofa with the padded, rolled arms. Because she was a teacher, several cloth bags spilling worksheets and lesson plans, rested on the floor in the short hallway leading to the front door.

"I was glad when you came by the school this morning." Bertie placed her mug carefully on the coffee table.

"Yeah, it's always good to see you." Lacey leaned back and crossed her legs. Her cheek touched one of Bertie's crocheted afghans, and she had the urge to snuggle into its warmth. She restrained herself and instead smiled warmly at her friend.

"Hey," Bertie exclaimed. "You know better than to look at me that way."

Lacey grinned, eyes sparkling. "What way?"

Bertie smoothed her short blond hair. "Okay, okay. I'm going to check on the pizza."

"Bring me another beer?"

A noncommittal grunt floated back to her, as Bertie made her way to the kitchen.

After talking with her briefly at Ryan Nash Elementary, Bertie had invited Lacey over for dinner, where they could have a proper discussion, one not surrounded by noisy, distracting children. Lacey had agreed, as long as she could bring a veggie pizza. A real coup, because Lacey had become vegetarian during her college years at Coves Community, and Bertie had never embraced the lifestyle.

"Almost ready. I turned the oven off. Here you go," Bertie said, handing Lacey a beer.

"You're getting thin. I thought we were supposed to get chunkier as we got older," Lacey remarked.

"Ah, well," Bertie slanting her eyes to one side. "I've been on this health kick. Been going over to the Circuit a couple days a week."

"Ha!" Lacey laughed and almost snorted beer from her nose. She choked but recovered. "Got any classes under Moe?"

Bertie screwed up her nose. "Moe Mosser? Of course."

A smile crawled across her lips as she gleaned Lacey's meaning. "Ah, you're talking about him and Bonnie. I don't know but they sure do spend a lot of time all smiley-flirty. Gets annoying."

"Sure you aren't jealous?"

"Hell, no. He's not my type, as you well know, Miss Thing." She nudged Lacey with one stockinged toe.

"Oh, yes. I remember that well."

Lacey's thoughts flew back to when she and Bertie had been a hot and heavy item. Miss Roberta Madison was quite the passionate person, and Lacey had been head over heels for her. Briefly. Then life had interfered, with Bertie accepting the job as a teacher. Becoming an elementary school teacher in gossipy Queens Lot had dampened their passion, and Bertie had, oh, so genteelly stepped back into the closet. Lacey couldn't fault her. Being a teacher in a small town is like wearing a red target on your back. Being a lesbian for either of them—at least openly—was pretty much out of the question.

"You know, you probably will have to like, meet a guy and get married one day. Otherwise people will continue to talk," Lacey mused, resting her chin on the rim of her beer bottle.

Bertie shook her head firmly in the negative. "Being a spinster is just fine and dandy with me. They can all go pound sand for all I care."

"Bert, you know I'm right," Lacey insisted softly.

"Well, what about you, sugar?" Bertie cocked her head to one side and studied her friend. "You need to settle down yourself. People here talk about you, as well."

"I know," Lacey said with a deep sigh. "Think Mom and Dad would be okay if I brought a woman home?"

They both pondered the idea in silence, until Bertie abruptly let loose a bark of laughter. "Oh yeah, right!"

Lacey bristled. "I don't know. They might. I mean, what else am I supposed to do? The men in this town carry boxes of rocks on top of their necks. I've made no secret how I feel about them."

"Boston marriage? You wanna move in here with me?" Bertie laughed. "Wanna be roomies? Friends without benefits?"

Lacey frowned. "Have you looked at yourself? At me? No way would we pass if we moved in together. How about we just leave well enough alone?"

Bertie rose and brought back plates of pizza slices warm from the oven. She handed one to Lacey. "Two for me, two for you."

Lacey accepted the plate eagerly. "It's a start, I guess."

"Well, I'm stopping at two," Bertie declared.

Both women moaned upon tasting the first bite. "What does our man Early do to these pizzas that make them so damned good?" Lacey asked.

"Probably lard," Bertie responded, studying her piece.

Lacey nodded, eyebrows raised. "Could be. The crispy mushrooms are good, huh?"

"You know, we could date again. On the sly, like tonight. I mean, if you wanted."

Lacey didn't respond right away, waiting until their plates were mostly empty. "It wouldn't be right, Bert. If I were going to be in a relationship with you..." She lifted her eyes and looked at Bertie. Bertie gasped softy, deeply affected by that gaze. "I'd want to shout it from the courthouse clock tower. I'd want everyone to know."

Bertie swallowed and lowered her gaze. Those blue eyes of Lacey's—they'd always torn at her. So goddamned sexy, so goddamned clear. It just wasn't fair what those eyes did to her. Viscerally *and* emotionally. "Well, umm..."

Lacey set her plate aside and leaned forward to grasp Bertie's hand. She squeezed it meaningfully.

"It's okay, Bert. Things are...comfortable...the way they are now. I'm good with it. It's okay."

Bertie wondered if it was okay with her. She wanted Lacey in her life. She didn't want to be simply comfortable. She sighed and looked away again. It really was for the best. Sometimes reality had to win out over fantasy. "Yeah, I know what you mean." She turned a bright smile on Lacey. "It's all good."

Chapter Thirteen

A COLD FRONT HAD moved through, and Kenton shivered in the short denim jacket he was wearing. He leaned his weight on one foot and then the other, trying to warm the muscles of his legs. Maybe the rest stop outside Queens Lot wasn't the best place for picking up old guys. Mother had been specific though, and his training had been thorough as well as intense. He knew he was being tested. Still, it was cold and deserted here.

Just as he was fishing his car keys out of his pocket, he spied headlights approaching through the country darkness of I-17. As the lights moved closer, he made sure he could be seen in the glow from the sputtering street light high above him.

Sure enough, the driver of the small foreign car must have seen him, for the vehicle slowed and pulled into the parking area. Kenton didn't look at him, playing the nonchalant card, as the driver slowly got out and locked his car. He moved off in the direction of the soda vending machine. Kenton could hear the thunk as the canned soda hit the bottom tray. Still, he studied the small patch of forest off to his right. A moment later, he heard the car's automatic locks then the driver's door closed. The ignition started smoothly. As expected, the car rolled slowly in his direction. Only then did he look directly at the driver. Kenton knew this game well.

The window lowered as the driver pulled up alongside Kenton. "Get in," the driver ordered. "I have rum and coke. You must be freezing."

Kenton studied the young face looking up at him. It wasn't anybody he recognized, but that was not surprising. Most guys didn't cruise their local rest stops. He studied the young man's handsome face for several seconds, tempted, of course. It was not his mission for the evening, however.

"I can't," he replied finally. "I'm waiting for someone. Thanks for the offer though."

The young man frowned in confusion, unsure if he should persist. Kenton helped him with that. "No, really, I can't. Not tonight. Maybe I'll run into you again sometime. A better time."

He seemed to understand that Kenton was serious this time, and with a small wave, he raised his window and pulled back onto the interstate.

"Come back by in about thirty years, numbnuts," Kenton muttered. He strolled slowly toward the front doors of the rest stop. It wasn't open twenty-four seven, but at least there was some shelter in the alcove where the vending machines were. He wished he'd asked the cruiser for a drink of rum. He sure needed something to warm him up. He again debated leaving. Maybe he'd try the Three Pigs.

Another car was approaching, from the opposite direction this time. Kenton didn't bother stepping into the light so he could be seen, remaining in the shelter of the alcove. The driver of the long, expensive sedan must have seen him anyway, for the car slowed, then pulled vertically into one of the parking slots. The driver sat inside a good three minutes, obviously assessing the scene.

It was a lone figure and Kenton couldn't tell whether it was male or female. He acted like he was awaiting someone, eyes turned toward the highway. If it was a woman, she'd be worried about her safety alone with this young man. If it was a man, well, then, obviously, he was cruising for a good time. A moment of fear gripped him. Suppose it was a man, a violent man who could hurt him?

He shook that off, glancing at the surrounding trees. He was safe.

Presently, the car door opened with a solid click of the disengaging lock and a very well-dressed, distinguished older man stepped from the driver's seat. He was wearing a stylish, camel-colored trench coat, probably made of wool. He'd loosened his tie and the top button of his oxford shirt. He stood there, five feet from Kenton.

"Can you tell me how I get to Mobile from here," he asked, eyes checking Kenton out.

Kenton simpered in what he knew was an adorable fashion. He took one step toward the man and pointed. "You just keep on south on seventeen until you come to the junction of sixty-five and I-10. You'll want to take ten east. It's not too far once you get there."

"Thank you," the elegant man said. "You look mighty cold out there. Why don't you get in my car for a spell and warm up?"

Kenton tried on a worried air. "Are you sure? I mean, I don't want to be any trouble..."

The older man smiled, and Kenton fell a little in love with him, just a little. Kenton smiled back and scurried around to the passenger side. Inside, the heater was on full bore and Kenton relished in it, rubbing his hands together and turning the passenger air vents his way.

"So, what's your name and why are you out here in this cold? Don't you know winter's coming?" His chiding tone was amused so Kenton just chuckled and shook his head.

"Yep. Guess I'm not the smartest tool in the toolbox," he said deprecatingly. He extended his hand. "I'm Kenny."

"Talbot," the man said, taking Kenton's hand. "Nice to meet you."

"And you." Kenton released the older man's hand but not before his thumb moved sensuously against the back of that hand. "Are you traveling for business or for pleasure?"

Talbot shrugged. "A little of both. I'm heading to Mobile for a marketing presentation."

"Marketing? Is that sort of like advertising?" Kenton was finally beginning to thaw, and a warm glow of nervous anticipation was beginning to fill him.

Talbot laughed low in his throat. "Yes, you could say that. Soooo, are you waiting for someone? Is that why you were standing out in the cold?"

Kenton smiled brightly. "I think I was waiting for you."

Again that low, sexy laugh but, surprisingly, it caused Talbot to lean forward and cough uncontrollably. In the slanting light from the street lamp, Kenton saw that Talbot was older than he'd originally thought.

"Hey, man, are you okay?"

Talbot nodded. "Don't worry, nothing contagious. Bum ticker. Makes it hard to catch my breath sometimes."

Kenton slid closer, as he fished a silver flask from

his coat pocket. "Here, have a sip of this. Great tonic for when you're under the weather."

His body language was relaxed and welcoming as he unscrewed the cap. Talbot smiled and rested one palm on Kenton's thigh. "You're a sweet boy, aren't you?"

Kenton wriggled with happiness. "I try, Mister T, I try. But maybe you can tell me just how sweet I am."

Talbot took the flask and sniffed it. "Bourbon?"

"Black label, baby. Only the finest."

Talbot took a pull on the flask. "Ahh, that's good. Now, where were we?"

Kenton laughed and extended his neck toward Talbot. "You were going to kiss me on the neck...right here."

A fleeting shadow passed through the glow from the streetlamp outside, and Kenton knew that the angels had gathered outside the car. He closed his eyes and felt something akin to sexual release as Talbot slumped against him.

Chapter Fourteen

THE FOREVER REST FUNERAL Home was located at the western end of Hawthorne Street. It was a long, low ranch-style building with an extensive basement for storing and preparing the bodies for burial or cremation. Although Lacey had never been down there, Sully had and he'd described it as a cold, utilitarian, yet ultimately creepy area.

No one was immediately evident when Lacey stepped inside, and the only sound was the unassuming creak of her duty belt. She'd actually never been inside the funeral home while in uniform. It was a new experience for her. She strode slowly along the wide central aisle, peering curiously into the empty receiving rooms as she moved along. Services were sometimes held in these elegant rooms upstairs. Lacey was always impressed by the subtle comfort the sterile but well-designed rooms offered.

"Hello?" she said finally, her voice a strident whisper. "Anyone home?" She knew that Bobby's wife, Kasey, sometimes helped out at the funeral home, but she didn't appear to be working today. Unless, of course, she was downstairs, helping with Maureen's body.

Lacey moved to the right and entered a plush viewing room, decorated in garnet-colored brocade and rich burgundy velvet. There was an open coffin at the front, in a curtained-off alcove and, God help her, she had to go see if anyone was inside. She moved gingerly forward, noting how shiny the white satin interior appeared in the overhead spot lighting. Her mind seemed to be firing aimlessly, as fear catapulted throughout her being. She tried to squelch it. After all, she was the sheriff of both Coves County and the town of Queens Lot.

She stopped just at the alcove and peered in. Sudden sadness filled her. It actually swamped her. Inside, lay the body of young, not yet eighteen, Ronda Walls. Sully had covered the horrific car crash that took her life. A couple of boomerang thugs had stolen a car, and Sully had answered the call. On the way to the crime scene, he spotted the crook's vehicle and gave chase. The stolen car crashed into the car driven by Ronda's mother, Sue. She and Ronda had been on their way to the grocery store. Sue survived. Ronda did not.

Now, as Lacey looked down at the resting corpse, she saw none of the horrific details Sully had shared about Ronda's death. In fact, Clevon had somehow masterfully hidden the fact that Ronda's left arm had been shattered by slamming into the steering column. And by keeping the bottom half of the casket closed, he prevented anyone from ever guessing at the condition of the young victim's legs.

Lacey leaned forward. Ronda really did look as though she were sleeping, as though no violence had touched her. Clevon had really...Lacey abruptly jerked backward. Wait, had Ronda's eyes moved? She swallowed hard and backed away from the casket. Ronda was dead. Yes, and she would stay that way. Lacey chuckled weakly, as she exited through the door on her left. It was a good thing she didn't get creeped out from places like this. Well, not much.

At the end of the center aisle, there was a heavy wooden door. She paused, wondering whether to knock. *Shit, this is a business*, she told herself mentally. A carpeted stairway greeted her, as she pulled the door open. "Hey, Clevon? Bobby? Anyone down there?"

She hoped to God no hoarse, death-slowed voices replied

"Hey, Lacey, come on down," Clevon called brightly. "I'm in the prep room to the right."

Lacey quietly shut the heavy door and entered the depths of the funeral home. Clevon, wearing a white lab coat over his jeans and button-down shirt, was busily working on Maureen's body.

"I'm getting her mostly presentable. You know, for the family," Clevon said.

A sheet covered Maureen's naked, age-spot-speckled body. Her fleshy bare arms rested on top, and Lacey was surprised by the sight, realizing that she had never seen Miss Maureen in a short-sleeved blouse.

"Man, I bet she got hot while gardening," she muttered to herself.

"What's that?"

"Did you find anything unusual about the body?" She moved around to the other side of the table so she could see him better.

Clevon raised up from combing Maureen's hair and gave Lacey his full attention. "I did. I admit I was reluctant to compare any of the recent deaths, but her body was just like Ronnie's and like Carrie Moss's before him. I checked my notes, and they all had pinpoint pupils and slack muscles."

"How abnormal is that?"

"Well." He placed a finger on his chin as he mulled her question. "The body usually stiffens in about two hours after death, although some bodies go a few hours past that. This condition seems to delay that for many hours. It's definitely significant."

"And the eyes. What's that about?" Lacey studied his face as she awaited his answer. His short, dark hair, straight as a board, stuck up a little in back. *Very Alfalfa-esque,* she thought.

"Generally, the eyes will dilate at the moment of death, due to lack of muscle ability, of course. Occasionally, they'll pinpoint up again when rigor sets in. This case, in particular, makes no sense because rigor is delayed and the pupils aren't relaxed."

"That's strange." Her radio squawked static, and she switched the button off. "Is it drugs, maybe? I mean, I know these elderly people don't fit the druggie demographic, but what if someone else is doing it to them?"

Clevon sighed and walked to a nearby desk. "I don't have the other bodies any more, but I did a preliminary tox test on Maureen here. Nothing flagged, so I'm not sure what it could be." He lifted a prepackaged test kit and handed it to Lacey. As he had indicated, none of the dots of her blood had triggered a color change on the chart.

"Damn," Lacey muttered. "Not going to be easy to get to the bottom of this thing, Clevon."

"Maybe it's not really a thing? Just an unfortunate string of coincidental deaths?"

"That could be. Guess my gut is just getting in the way."

Clevon giggled and the sound struck Lacey as highly incongruous in the surgical-suite-like, all-metal prep room. She raised an eyebrow.

"You know...gut." He chuckled briefly then stifled his merriment.

"Umhm," Lacey said, staring at Maureen. "If someone were to poison them...what would he use? And how?" She turned her gaze on Clevon. "Did you see any injection sites when you washed them?"

Clevon shook his head. "Nope, nothing noticeable. And I have no idea what drug would cause the signs I'm seeing. And I know most drugs. None of it makes sense."

"Okay," Lacey said with a long, drawn-out sigh. "Guess I'm looking for frogs when I got toads." She turned toward the doorway.

"So, what should I do now? You know, with the deceased."

"Her son is on his way here. I guess he'll decide. You can release her to him."

Clevon touched Maureen's hair, tidying a few wayward strands. "I hope he'll want an open casket. She looks pretty, doesn't she?"

Lacey was studying Clevon and getting a little creeped out by the funeral director. He was looking at Maureen so lovingly. Well, Lacey sure hoped Clevon wasn't doing anything...distasteful with the dead people of Queens Lot. She hitched up her belt. "Yep, you did a real good job there, Clevon. She looks nice."

He lifted his gaze back to Lacey. "Thanks, Sheriff. I appreciate that. You know, dealing with the subject of death or bodies almost every day, you've really got to learn to find beauty wherever you can. It's a small thing, you know, the makeup, making sure the features look lifelike, the hair. It's also much easier to do with these peaceful deaths. Violent deaths—well, we won't even go into how much work they are."

"Well, you're welcome. And Ronda upstairs looks real nice, too."

"Thanks, Lacey."

Silence fell, and Lacey shifted nervously. "Well, I'm gonna go to the office, so I'll see you later. Don't take this wrong, but I hope it'll be a while."

Clevon laughed lightly. "Yeah, I get that." He bent back to prettying the body. "Take care of yourself."

Lacey studied his actions one more time, as she made her way to the doorway. She knew that if she ever saw any evidence of him disrespecting or acting inappropriately with a body, she'd throw his ass in jail without a qualm.

Pondering the information Clevon had shared with her, Lacey drove slowly along Hawthorne, heading toward the station. This feeling she had about the deaths of the elderly was probably hogwash. Completely unsubstantiated so far. She seriously wished that they hadn't released Ronnie without a tox panel, but it was too late for that. Maybe it really was over. Maybe it was some weird coincidence that would soon end.

Chapter Fifteen

MOL MUST HAVE BEEN in a particularly bad mood most of the day, because when Debra got in at nine that evening after working late, Mol mostly gave her stink eye and cold shoulder. Debra, noticing the attitude, shrugged and moved down the hallway. Daisy followed her, tail wagging, but Debra didn't have it in her to be nice to the mutt.

"Go on. Get on with your fool self," she mumbled, as she keyed and turned each of the deadbolts. She shut the door in the expectant dog's face then relocked the locks. She slung her bag onto the bed and stepped into the bathroom to rinse her hands and splash cold water on her face.

She stared at her reflection and winced at how ordinary she looked. Short, dishwater-blond hair; nondescript hazel eyes, puffy at present, probably from too much salt in her diet; and a pudgy, jowly face more like her mother's than she appreciated.

She sighed. One of her online suitors, RedJenkies24, wanted to meet her in person. Not that it was likely to happen, thank goodness, as he was located on the other side of the state. The problem was that he thought she lived over there, as well. So now, she had to make up some believable excuse to avoid meeting him.

She left the bathroom and sat solidly on the edge of her bed. Life wasn't much to her liking lately. Even her online romances had soured. She had to keep jumping from virtual lover to virtual lover because most wanted to possess her in the real world, something that could never happen. For so many reasons. Everything seemed so pointless at the moment.

Fetching her cigarettes from the nearest desk, she lit one and inhaled the comforting smoke. She had been jonesing for one. Dapper Dan wouldn't let his employees smoke, even outside the store during their breaks. Said it looked bad.

She knew she should get on the computer and make up an excuse to tell RedJenkies24, but she just wasn't in the mood. It was a testament to how fucked up things were in her head right now. Usually, she was eager to go online and play with her chat friends.

The television volume increasing from the living room didn't help her mindset. Obviously, Mol was trying real hard to piss Debra off. She leaned and stubbed out her cigarette, anger swelling deep inside. She sat there a moment longer listening to the loud TV, but finally stood and changed her clothes, putting on comfortable sweat pants and a T-shirt, slipping her feet into plastic clogs. She unlocked and relocked her door then strode down the hall into the living room.

"That's too loud, Mama. Can you turn it down just a little?" She tried to keep a civil tone even though anger was seething through her.

"You forgot my goddamn bath and my hair," Mol said loudly. "You don't give one flying shit about me. Not no way, not no how, and I'm sick of it. Sick of it, you hear?"

Debra paused in thought. Fuck. It was the day

she'd promised to wash and cut her mother's hair. "I'm sorry," she said finally, sullenly. "But I just got home, all right? Give me a minute to get settled in, for Christ's sake."

"You forgot, just go on and admit it." Mol watched her with jaundiced, alcohol blurred eyes.

Debra nodded as she moved toward the master bedroom and bathroom. "I did, I'm not gonna lie to you, but it was mostly because I forgot what day it was."

She stretched and pushed the shower curtain to one side then went back into the living room to help her mother rise from her chair. Mol was quiet, as they made their way through the bedroom and into the small bath, only grunting a bit from the effort. Debra was thinking how much she hated this haircut ritual but knew it was unavoidable, like a bad menstrual period, one that happened every six weeks or so.

Mol sat on the edge of the bathtub and handed her cane to Debra who placed it to one side. Slowly, laboriously, Mol rolled each of her heavy stockings down her legs until they were nylon doughnuts. She handed them to Debra one at a time.

Fetching the cloth bag of hair cutting supplies, Debra brought them to the bathtub and laid them on the nearby toilet.

"Let's get that dress off," she said, leaning to pull the fabric out from under Mol's bottom. Soon, Mol was wearing only her panties and an old, yellowed slip. "I'll do your hair then see if we can't rustle up some supper."

"I want you to cut it real short this time, real close," Mol said, clacking her false teeth together.

Debra was taken aback. "Are you sure? You usually want it left a little longer."

Mol shook her head. "Botherin' me some. You just take it all off."

"Like down to about two inches all over?" Debra was still confused and perplexed at her mother's sudden change.

Mol swung one heel and it hit the side of the acrylic tub with a loud boom. "Stop askin' me stuff I done already tol' you, girl! Damn, you aggravatin'. Always have been."

Debra pressed her lips together and lifted her mother's legs until they were on the inside of the bathtub.

"Damn cold," Mol said.

"I'll get you a towel." Debra brought two towels, one to put between Mol's calves and the cold interior of the tub and another to wrap around her shoulders, to catch the hair.

Debra lifted Mol's comb from the sink and began to comb through Mol's dull, greasy hair. "I'm glad we're making it short," she began pleasantly. "It'll be easier to take care of."

Mol just grunted, and Debra reached for the haircutting shears. She'd gone ahead and bought a nice, sharp professional pair from the beauty shop at the strip mall just down the street. They'd cost all of twenty-five dollars, but that was okay. They got a good bit of use, because Debra used them to trim her own hair as well as to cut her mother's.

Using the comb, Debra divided out a thin hank of Mol's hair. She paused, preparing to ask Mol one more time if she wanted it super short. *Ah, hell with it*, she thought as she brought the scissors less than three inches from Mol's scalp. She snipped off a good eight inches of her mother's lank, graying hair. Then another length. A sense of joy filled her, as she relished the control she had been allowed. Oddly enough, bereft of its usual length and heaviness, Mol's hair began to curl a little as Debra moved from one side to the other. It was almost pretty. If it had been cleaner. She dropped the cutoff hanks of hair into the waste bin after each snip.

"I know what you do," Mol said suddenly, her voice low and hate laden. "You split tailin' it for them boys, ain't you?"

Debra sighed and her movements became more businesslike, as she endeavored to finish as quickly as possible. "I don't do any sucha thing, Mama, and you know it."

"I don't know nothin' of the kind. I hear you in there gigglin' on that phone of yours of a night. I know you got all them men thinkin' you is somethin'." She paused and scratched under one sagging breast, catching the material of the slip under that breast.

"You always was a hot ass, even shakin' that big ol' ass at my men. I know. I was watchin'. You thinkin' you got that old wool pulled over Mol's eyes. That's bullshit!" She slammed one hand against the tub, making a new echoing boom fill the room.

"Yeah, Mama, you just go on tellin' yourself that. I'm sure it makes you sleep easy at night." Debra finished up the haircut, just leaving it parted in the middle. Earlier, she had played with the idea of wispy bangs, but she didn't have to continue listening to her mother's hatefulness. She certainly didn't *want* to. She'd just draw her bath and let her soak while she got some food together. Hell, maybe she'd do them all a favor and drown in it.

Smiling at her humor, Debra leaned to punch in the

rubber stopper, but her mother grabbed her neck from behind. It was a surprisingly tight grip and caught Debra totally by surprise. Mol leaned close and spat words into her daughter's ear.

"Shake that ass all you want. Ain't nobody ever gonna want anything you got. You're pure dee ugly and everyone knows it. Ain't worth a damn, ain't never gonna be."

A low rumble grew somewhere deep in Debra. She felt blood rush madly into the veins of her face, even as she realized that the rumble was a growl of hatred coming from the deepest recesses of her being. The growl continued to grow, as the hand holding the scissors swung backward and caught Mol under the chin.

Chapter Sixteen

"LACEY, WE GOT ANOTHER one," Sully said, as soon as she got out of the county cruiser Wednesday morning. It looked as though he'd been standing outside the building, just waiting for Lacey to get to work.

"Damn!" she muttered, as she narrowed her eyes at him. "Old?"

Sully nodded. "Rightly so. And Clevon pulled his medicals. Heart trouble."

She stared pensively at her shiny black shoes. "Maybe it was a heart issue then."

"Maybe. Clevon didn't say either way. Said he died last night."

She sighed, thinking about the coffee pods waiting inside. "Guess I'll go see him. Where's the body?"

"Still out at the rest stop south of town. He said to tell you to come out and release the body yourself. Said he'd wait on you." Sully squinted his deep-set eyes.

"Wanna ride?" Lacey asked, as she climbed back into the cruiser.

Sully nodded emphatically, as he hurried around to the passenger side.

"If I pull up over at The Bean, will you run in and get us both a tall one?" she asked as she flipped the visor up.

"Sure, sure," Sully answered. "Cold or hot today?"

She pulled her wallet from her back pocket and passed it to him. "I'm thinking hot. Fish out a ten for me, would you?"

He complied and returned the wallet to her just as they pulled next to the sidewalk in front of Ellen DeMalley's coffee shop, The Bean. This was an old routine, and she knew Sully would never openly thank her for buying his morning coffee. And that was okay. He was a good, faithful employee making federal minimum wage with three kids and a wife at home. Charity didn't set well with him, however, so they just never mentioned it.

She waited, tapping her fingernails on the faux-leather-wrapped steering wheel. She studied the pedestrian traffic along Hawthorne and Oak and was glad to see that all looked normal. These deaths though, they were bugging her in a big way.

The heady scent of freshly ground and brewed coffee preceded Sully's return. She took the nectar of the morning from him gratefully and blew halfheartedly into the opening before taking that first glorious, scalding sip. Sure, she could have had coffee at home or even the office, but barista-steamed milk and her usual two sugars made for a heavenly concoction that she adored.

After the euphoria had abated, she turned to Sully. "You know, this thing with all the old people dying is really getting to me."

Sully nodded in his slow, slightly dopey manner. "It just doesn't make any sense. How can anyone wrap his head around it? Old folks are fixin' to die anyway, why hurry up the whole thing?"

"Exactly! And I think that's what's getting on my last nerve...the senselessness of it." She placed her tall to-go cup in the console holder and started the cruiser, slamming it into gear. "And I'll tell you right now, I'm getting a little hot under the collar. If someone thinks they can just come into our little town and do away with all our salty or sweet old people, well, they just better get a new idea."

Lacey meandered the cruiser through town, listening to Sully verbally list the most recent deaths of the elderly and even some of the younger ones before she pulled out onto the highway and traveled down Route 17 toward Chatom.

The Paulsen Briggs Rest Stop loomed on the right, and Lacey pulled in and parked next to a tan and brown Cadillac. There were no other cars in this part of the lot, but she could spy two employee cars parked out back.

Clevon and Bobby hovered near the wide-open, driver-side door. Frank, on day shift this week, hunkered down below, sweeping something from the wheel well into a plastic evidence bag. Two state employees hovered in the covered entryway. The older of them held the fingers of one hand spread over her mouth, the other arm wrapped around her waist as if for comfort. The man craned his neck to see what was going on by the vehicle.

Lacey sighed and lifted her coffee to take with her. No way was she letting this magnificent, necessary cuppa get cold.

"Hey, Clevon. I see we have another one," she said as she approached. "What the hell is going on around here?"

"Well, hold on, Lacey. He did have a bad heart and it was failing, according to the literature about him." There was a doubtful cast to his eyes that made Lacey question his statement.

"But? What did you find, Clevon?"

The medical examiner aspect of Clevon tugged at his spiky hair. "It's the same as the others, Sheriff. We got the limp muscles, the constricted pupils...all of it. I've just never seen the like."

Bobby watched his boss cautiously, as he slowly unfolded a brown plastic body bag. Lacey shooed him aside and saw that there was a handsome older man, a stranger, slumped back in the curved leather seat. He was wearing a long, tan coat over a business suit. He looked peaceful.

"He'd been drinking, too. I smelled something on his lips so I swabbed them," Clevon said, helping Bobby with the bag.

"Do you see his hands?" Lacey said. She rested her hand holding the coffee on the top of the car so she could lean in a bit farther. "They're folded...like someone put them that way."

Again, Clevon argued the point with a shake of his head. "He had heart failure, and sometimes that can be a slow death, just not able to get a breath in to oxygenate your lungs. It might have been that way."

"No," Lacey was shaking her head, "He would have struggled, fought for air. This seems different."

Clevon shrugged. "Maybe. Can we take him on back now? Sun's getting hot out here."

"Yeah, the vampires gotta get on back before they turn to ash," Sully joked, waving his fingers in a creepy manner.

"Get a life," Bobby muttered, as he handed Lacey the clipboard so she could sign over the body.

The two men, with Sully's help, managed to get the elderly man into the body bag and into the back of Clevon's van. Clevon waved once, and then pulled the lumbering van out onto the highway, heading north.

"Here's his personal effects," Sully said, moving around to the passenger side.

"Yeah, wallet was in his pocket and registration was in the glove box. It's his car. Name's Talbot Spence. Business cards say he worked for an advertising company up Birmingham way."

"Long way from home," Lacey muttered. She took a deep draught of coffee and followed Sully around to the passenger side. She lifted the evidence bag of possessions. There was a long, sleek wallet, a leather business card holder, keys on a chromed, initialized ring, a signet pinkie ring and a gold-plated pen.

"This is money talking," she said. "Hey, is there money in the wallet?"

"Nope. Running on empty. Credit cards all seem to be there, though." Frank was packing all the evidence into large paper grocery bags. "I went through the suitcase in the trunk. Nothing but clothes and bathroom stuff."

A loud rattle announced the arrival of Booker Nash and his bright yellow tow truck. Frank walked toward the truck, and using hand motions, began guiding him backward toward the victim's car.

"I tell you, Sully. I'm not liking this one bit," Lacey said, absently sipping coffee. Her eyes scanned the car, the parking lot, the vending machines, as she tried to envision what had happened there the night before. *Had someone been lying in wait? A hitchhiker? Was it an assignation gone bad?* But no matter how hard her eyes scanned the surroundings, she could pick nothing out that might give her a clue. Concrete sidewalks, a solid brick building that had certainly been locked last night, streetlamps that lit the area well. Determined to find something out, Lacey stolidly approached the rest stop employees, tossing the half-empty cup of coffee into the trash bin. It had suddenly lost its appeal.

Chapter Seventeen

STEPPING BACK IN HORROR, Debra peered around to see the damage. Blood was coursing down the front of Mol's slip. Her brown eyes were open wide in disbelief, as was her mouth, and through the opening between her lips, Debra could see the scissor blade junction at the back of the mouth cavity.

Debra grinned and a slight chuckle escaped her. "Well. Ain't you a sorry sight?"

Mol's arms moved chaotically, and grunting sounds emanated from her mouth.

"Oh, you want that taken out, I guess. Here, lemme see what I can do."

Turning and pushing Mol away with her left hand, she used the right hand to yank the scissors from her mother's neck. More blood gushed forth with an odd, lingering gurgle, and Mol raised both hands to hold her throat. She watched Debra with terrified eyes.

"What? You got nothin' to say now, bitch?" Debra looked at the scissors' bloody blades and then back at her mother. "I got plenty to say."

She held the scissors tightly and shoved the blades deep into Mol's chest. They glanced off bone but then sank deeply, satisfyingly deeply, into the soft flesh. Mol looked down then back up at Debra. Debra smiled at her and pulled the blades free, allowing a new fount of blood to appear.

"Like how you're a *shit* of a mother. A damn bitch dog could have done a better job than you." She pushed the blades in again, lower this time. The flesh was softer there, even more satisfying.

"Like how you let your nasty men friends *rape* me while pretendin' it was somethin' I caused." She pulled the blades free and punched them in again, into the soft pillows of Mol's lower abdomen.

"Like, I gotta say...who's ugly now, bitch?" she whispered right into her mother's face.

Mol's eyes rolled back, and she fell forward into the basin of the bathtub. Debra jerked to one side to get out of the way. Blood still poured freely, and soon Mol was a study in red and white, curled in a fetal position at the bottom of the cream-toned tub.

Debra stood beside the tub, chest heaving. She giggled and then chuffed as though alarmed. "So, I gotta say...again. Who's ugly now?"

She looked down at her bloody hand, still holding the shears, and immediately dropped the weapon on top of her mother's body.

"No, no, no," she muttered in a low monotone. "No, no, no."

A sound at the door startled her, and she turned to see both dogs fidgeting in the bathroom doorway. Duff, the big black lab mix, ran his tongue over his muzzle nervously, even as he danced, looking at Debra. Daisy, the little shih tzu mix, took a defensive stance while watching Debra warily.

Debra started to be hateful to them, as was her wont, but knowing her karma was already in deep jeopardy, she spoke softly as she approached the door. "It's all right, doggies. No need to worry."

She shut the door and turned back to the body, her mother, lying still and finally quiet in the bathtub.

"Shit. Shit, shit, shit." A short bark of laughter escaped her, and she placed both hands over her mouth. "Ain't this a fucking pickle?"

Debra grabbed a towel from a nearby towel rack and spread it across Mol's body. She looked at her hands then moved quickly to the sink and washed them and her face in a lengthy meditative process. She made sure the nails were clean and that all the water running down the drain was crystal clear—no soap or blood evident. She carefully dried those hands then left the room, snapping off the light and shutting the door.

The dogs awaited her, still manifesting nervousness. She spoke to them desultorily, as she led them through the master bedroom and to the kitchen door. She opened it and let them out into the yard.

In the small front room, she sat in Mol's usual chair and lit a cigarette. The television was still on, so she lowered the volume. It was tuned to an evening news program. She rubbed a hand across her face and thought about herself being a hot topic on the evening news for killing her mother. How could she explain what had just happened? It was like she was watching it from afar. She certainly had no intention of...well, there was nothing to be done now. She breathed a sigh of what she soon realized was relief. No more Mol to do daily battle with. That could be a very good thing.

She drew deeply on the cigarette and choked as a sudden, unexpected thought attacked her. Coughing out acrid smoke, she leapt to her feet, eyes so wide they hurt. What had she done? She had taken a life without consecration. Again! She sat down slowly. Mother would be horrified and...and angry!

Debra tapped her feet, clogs echoing loudly in the incredibly still house. Her fingers twitched at the cigarette. No, there was no way she could allow Mother to find out about this. It went against everything the angels believed and if she knew that Debra was capable of such a heinous act...well, there was no telling what could happen.

She stubbed out the cigarette and rose to pace thoughtfully. And people would ask questions eventually. Mol would be missed by someone. John, her drinking buddy, came by to visit about once a month. She hugged herself, mouth open in a silent cry of misery. What the fuck had she done? She physically and mentally shook herself.

"Get a grip," Debra told herself aloud.

First things first. She needed to get rid of the body. She tried to calm her galloping thoughts. What was the best way to dispose of that much...flesh? The angels always left their offerings in a respectful stance, as dictated by their ritual. This was...desecration. She paused and hung her head. Desecration. Disrespect. Yes, her mother had been a bitch and a schemer, but every life taken deserved respect. And ritual.

Lifting her chin, she suddenly knew what she had to do. A sense of clarity sharpened her stance and her thoughts. First and foremost—hide—no, dispose of— the body. This would require more thought, maybe some research on the Web. But one thing was certain; Mother must never know about this.

Secondly, she needed to create a paper trail that would explain her mother's absence. This, too, would require some thought. Surely there was someone, somewhere who others would believe could want Mol staying with them—in a fictional way.

Scratching and whining at the kitchen door brought Debra's attention back to the present. She had completely forgotten about the dogs. She sighed. This was another loose end she needed to tie up.

"Come on in, mutts," she said, as she held the door open for them. She fed them dry kibble absently, as she made mental lists. It could be done. She knew that British murderer John Haigh disposed of his bodies. With acid, if memory served her. Ted Bundy left bodies in the woods, and Dahmer ate them. Ridgeway buried them and Gein made useful household items from his victims.

She shook her head and opened the refrigerator. She pulled out a partial piece of cheese and took it to the wooden cutting board on the counter. She pulled a knife from the magnetic rack and sliced off three large rectangles. Methodically, she wrapped the remaining cheese, placed it back in the refrigerator, and snagged a bottle of beer before closing the door.

Yes, it could be done. She just needed to learn from the experts. She headed toward her bedroom and her beloved computers.

Chapter Eighteen

THE ABIDING LOVE BAPTIST Gathering, a storefront church mainly for the homeless, was oddly devoid of chitchat Sunday morning as the few, mostly downtrodden congregants filed in. The Gathering was a relatively new church that had sprung up near a vacant lot in downtown Queen's Lot. A bright sandwich board outside welcomed one and all.

Excited to have found the church, Bathsheba hummed along with the light music and her hands played an imaginary piano as she made her way along the center aisle. About one quarter of the way in, she spied him. Quickly, she slid into the battered, recycled pew next to him. He lifted his eyes and looked at her. His dark-brown eyes were rheumy and yellow, and she could tell that he had seen enough pain in this life. A cannula over his ears and in his nostrils carried oxygen from the surprisingly small machine sitting on the floor at his feet.

Impulsively, Bathsheba took his hand and entwined their fingers. She studied the hands, noting how his skin was a lighter brown than hers. His hands were stained and callused, and she could tell he'd worked hard all his life. She lifted her eyes and put all the compassion she felt into the gaze she shared with him. He smiled tremulously and did not pull his hand away.

"Be seated, brothers and sisters," the preacher said. "God's love has filled me today, and I just need to let it out, let it out."

A spate of laughter ran around the room, and a couple amens sounded. Bathsheba turned her attention to the podium, as she settled in next to the oxygen man. The minister was a tall, black man wearing a spiffy single-breasted suit. His hair was closely cropped, and he had a small, black mustache. He was very handsome, and Bathsheba admired his very straight posture.

She had a thing about posture, making sure that her own posture was upright by often walking with a stack of books balanced atop her head. Her mother had taught her that when she was just a little girl growing up in southeast Queens Lot. That was years before her mother pulled the trigger of the shotgun that blew her head off. Bathsheba knew a secret about that. She knew why her mother had pulled that trigger, though she never told anyone. It was because that man, Bathsheba's father, that minister, had come to their house that very same day and said that there was no way Mama's girl-child could be his. Everyone knew that he would never cheat on his beautiful, Godly wife. He'd left then, and Bathsheba's mother rocked to and fro on the sofa for hours, tears streaming down her face.

Bathsheba had tried everything she could to stem the tears, and she would never forget her feeling of helplessness in that moment. She had fetched Mama's special bottle and patted her shoulder as she drank from it. Later, the gun sound woke her from a deep sleep. The first thing she noticed was that her mother's best dress, and her almost perfect posture, had been ruined forever.

After this, in an effort to honor her mother's

valuable teachings, Bathsheba had practiced her posture every day, even though her foster brothers and sisters had made fun. She was also very careful about what she ate and about removing body hair. And she continued to follow earnestly in her mother's religion, attending church whenever she could.

"I think we should start with a hymn, though, get the old blood moving." The minister turned to the pianist. "EllaRae, can you start us off, please? Everyone, let's stand and greet our neighbor as we sing." He broke out into a loud, proud rendition of "Amazing Grace," as the small congregation stood and greeted one another.

The man next to her winced once as the tiny needle entered his thigh, but after absently rubbing the spot, he turned away and hugged his neighbor on the other side. Bathsheba tucked the tiny flattened pouch and needle into her Bible and pulled it close to her chest. She lifted her clear voice in song.

Chapter Nineteen

FUCKING HALLOWEEN. LACEY WATCHED the carrying on from the sheriff's department window and cringed inside. Children and teens milled outside that window, and Lacey knew that they were waiting to come inside for some of the candy that Erva gave away each year. Lacey had tried to dissuade her from giving candy out, but Erva stood her ground, saying that offering one more safe place for kids to get candy was a good thing. Lacey supposed it was good public relations.

She sighed and turned away from the pirates, ghosts, ghouls, and princesses cluttering the sidewalk. Hesitantly, she returned to the monsters in her computer.

Jeffrey Dahmer, the Milwaukee cannibal. She shuddered. Reading the blow by blow accounts of his crimes, she soon became horribly creeped out and, even more alarming, so overwhelmed so by his violence that she could no longer even register the horror of what he'd done.

Then there was Carlton Gary, the stocking strangler, who killed seven elderly women in Ohio. And John Thomas, The Southland Strangler, who had killed almost twenty people in California. She did a search on serial killers who target elderly people and found several in Spain, Mexico, Latvia, and quite a few in

America. Even women got into the act, someone named Dana Gray had killed three women just to rob them, and someone else had killed her patients in a nursing home. Disgusted, she flicked the page away and turned from her computer.

Lacey had decided that she definitely had a serial killer on her hands. Though Talbot Spence's death could have been from a bad heart, Lacey had a gut feeling that his death was proof of a murderer on the loose. Why else would someone fold his hands together? Make him appear peaceful? He looked posed, for fuck's sake, as did Maureen. She made a mental note to ask Clevon how Ronald had looked.

Her mind churned after two hours of reading about serial killers. Albert DeSalvo had posed his strangled bodies. Dennis Rader had as well. Could she have such a sinister character in Queen's Lot?

She felt a sudden need for company, so rose and moved out of her office. The main lobby of the department was a flurry of activity. Erva and Lloyd, witch and bigfoot respectively, were entertaining a group of young children.

"What do we have here?" Lacey intoned as she got close. She moaned and spread her arms in a spooky fashion, and two of the children squealed and giggled. A few others looked bored.

"Told you, you should have dressed up," Erva said.

Lacey lifted an eyebrow at her, as Lloyd shooed the treated children out the door.

"What? You think being a big, bad sheriff isn't scary? Just break the law one time, you'll see." Lacey loosened her disheveled hair fully and retied it into a ponytail with a coated rubber band.

"I'm really scared," Lloyd said in a smart alecky

way.

"Hmph. You should be. By the way, remind me again when curfew is. Shouldn't these kids be home in front of their video games or something?"

Erva stirred the big bowl of candy with one hand. "Lord, Lord. You do not like this holiday at all, do you?"

Lacey's attitude softened somewhat. "Oh, I don't know. I guess it has some merit. Kids do enjoy dressing up."

"I know I do," Erva said, adjusting her tall witch hat. "What other time do I get to act a little witchy?"

Lloyd pointedly cleared his throat, and Lacey laughed. She pulled at the fur covering him. "I bet that gets hot. It's in the seventies today."

"It rightly does," he said, tilting off the thick hood. "I sure could use something cold to drink." He took a seat next to Erva's desk.

Erva watched him a long moment then sighed and leaned to the small refrigerator beside her desk. She passed him a canned soda. Lacey cleared her throat, so Erva leaned and fetched two more. She passed one to Lacey then popped hers open just as Lloyd did. The sparkling, refreshing scent of caramel carbonation filled the air. Lacey moved to a nearby desk and pulled its chair over to Erva's desk. She took a seat and lifted her feet onto the metal rungs of Lloyd's chair.

"Your nanna okay?" Erva asked, as Lacey opened her soda. "She sure was in a way about Miss Maureen's passing."

Lacey nodded. "She's all right. Tough old coot. The thing that bugs her is that maybe it wasn't all that natural, you know?"

"I do know," Lloyd said in a low voice. "Somethin' just ain't right and you know it as well as I do, Sheriff."

Lacey nodded again. "You know, I think we might just have a serial killer on our hands."

Erva looked up from her soda. "Tell me you don't mean that."

"Oh, I do. Look at how it's adding up. And I'm not completely sure Alicee and Roy weren't killed that way, too."

"But that's too different," Lloyd said indignantly. "Weren't they stabbed?"

"That they were," Lacey replied. "But they were posed on the bed together. Who's to say it wasn't the start of it?"

"They weren't old though," Erva added. "The thing linking all these is that the...victims...are old people."

"When was the last time we had a murder like Alicee and Roy?" Lacey swung her feet down and leaned forward, soda can dangling from the hands between her knees.

"I bet it's been forty years or better since something happened like that," Lloyd mused.

"Exactly! And now here comes this horrible stabbing, just after their wedding day then, what? Maybe seven other people? I think I can count seven older people dead from so-called natural causes during this year alone."

"This Spence fellow," Erva said, nodding.

"Ronald and Maureen," Lloyd added.

"Remember Rebecca Ebsen? And there was old Olivia out Claremont Road," Erva said.

"And in January Doc Halpern's mama died. No one ever said what that was from," Lloyd added.

They fell silent, the sounds from the revelry outside penetrating.

The door swung open and a small devil appeared,

complete with pitchfork.

"Don't forget Carrie Moss this summer. She was healthy as a horse, even if she was old," Erva said, as she rose and took the bowl of candy toward the devil. He was soon joined by a ghost, a box of breath mints, and a cotton swab.

Lacey looked at Lloyd. "Holy cow," she mouthed.

Lloyd shrugged and pulled on his furry, cone-shaped hood.

Chapter Twenty

BATHSHEBA LOOKED AT MOTHER incredulously. "I honestly don't know. I left before the service completely finished."

Mother crossed her arms and sent Bathsheba waves of psychic disapproval. Angels were supposed to get to know their beloveds so that they can be sent on properly.

"Not the way, not the way," Danny muttered, as he stepped from foot to foot behind Mother.

Danny reached and took Bathsheba's hand, but she shook off his grasp. He whimpered quietly.

"He was really sick, even on oxygen," she said, closely studying the warped wooden floorboards of the Lawrence house. As an angel, she dreaded Mother's disapproval. "And I guess I got caught up in the moment. It was a beautiful service."

Mother looked askance at Danny but spoke to Bathsheba. "He could have fallen and been hurt. We don't treat our beloved ones that way." She sighed and let her arms drop to her sides. Slowly, she moved forward and embraced Bathsheba. "There, there, Angel. I know you didn't mean the gentleman any harm. We will hope he passed quietly there where he sat and that there were many there to honor his departure."

Bathsheba pulled back and lifted haunted dark

eyes to Mother. "I should have stayed there until he left, shouldn't I?"

Mother nodded grimly but took Bathsheba's hand in comfort. "You did the right thing, leaving him there, in this instance. It wouldn't do for the unbelievers to know about you, about us. So, it was the right decision. Next time, as I've taught you, make sure to be alone, and let another angel know so that the beloved can be properly honored and sent on their way."

Bathsheba hung her head even farther. "Yes, Mother. I promise to better honor our beloved in the future."

Mother forced a smile and lifted Bathsheba's head by cupping her chin. She looked into the other woman's eyes. "I know you will, precious angel. I have no doubt."

Bathsheba grinned in response and shivered as though in pleasure. Danny moved close, and the three wrapped their arms about one another and fell silent for a long time.

The slap of the screen door pulled Mother away, and she saw Debra enter, laptop in hand.

"Debra!" Danny said, acknowledging her presence. "Happy Halloween!"

"Hello, Danny, happy Halloween back to you." Debra placed the laptop on the kitchen table. She turned to Mother and the other angels. She looked rough, her blond hair unwashed and dark, bruise-like circles below each eye. Mother noted this, narrowing her eyes and seeking information. There was something about her mother again. Mother sighed. Poor, dear Debra. She had it rough at home.

"Hello, Angel," she said embracing Debra and pulling back to look deeply into her eyes. As expected, Debra smiled happily, and her countenance much improved.

"So, who is it?" she asked, turning away to open the lid of the laptop.

Mother pressed her lips together. "We don't know who he is," she admitted.

Debra slowly lowered the lid of the computer and glanced around the room, eyes landing on an embarrassed Bathsheba. "Ah, it's that way again."

"Afraid so. She got carried away."

She fixed her gaze on Mother. "But he needed peace, right?"

"Oh, yes," Bathsheba breathed out as she moved closer. She laid one palm on Debra's forearm. "He was very sick and very old."

Debra pressed her hand over Bathsheba's. "Well, that's good then. Right, Mother?" She turned to study Mother. The bell on the microwave dinged, and all of them turned toward the kitchen.

"There's lasagna from Early's, if anyone's hungry," Corey said, as he entered the dining room. He blew on his plate of food, as he took a seat at the table.

"Any traffic out there?" Mother asked Debra.

"No," Debra shook her head in the negative. "The trick or treaters don't usually come out this far. There weren't any cars on the road."

Mother nodded. "Good."

Corey looked up from his food, chewing. "I heard what happened, Sheba. I did that once, too, in the early days. The beloved was using a walker and oxygen. That was in..." He screwed up his forehead. "Mississippi, right, Mother?"

Mother sighed and took a seat at the table. She cupped her chin in one palm and leaned her weight on the tabletop. "Yes, I think it was." She shifted her long, black hair behind her shoulder.

"Talbot was beautiful," Kenton interjected, pulling up a vinyl-backed chair. "I really liked him."

Mother leaned and patted his hand. "I didn't get to meet him, but I'm sure he was lovely." She made eye contact with Kenton, sending approval.

"I was there. His passing was beautiful, wasn't it, Corey Angel?" Sarah said.

Corey nodded and chewed before answering. "We sent him off with prayers and chants for eternal, pain-free life."

Mother smiled and took in a deep breath. "See the difference, Bathsheba? Our way is love and peace, never uncertainty. Today was acceptable, but the right way is the better way. Do you see?" She turned to make a connection with Bathsheba.

"Yes, Mother. I understand." Bathsheba moved into the kitchen and began busily covering the food and putting it away. Mother knew she had a problem with food and eating.

"Sheba? Leave the food, Angel. Sarah Angel, get the box. It's time."

Sarah rose from the sofa and brought the box from the hidden compartment in one wall. They gathered around the low table, as Sarah laid out the candles.

"Louisiana," she said quietly on the fourteenth candle. Another rank was laid in place. Twenty-eight candles. "Texas," Sarah whispered. The next rank held twelve. "Arkansas," she said. Twenty-one candles. "Mississippi," she added. After the final rank of ten was laid, Sarah closed the lid on the box. "Alabama," she said as she began lighting them all, beginning with Louisiana.

The rest of the family watched reverently as each

candle flickered to life. "Tonight, we honor the passing of our unnamed beloved, who has finally found the freedom of everlasting peace. We honor all these souls who no longer suffer pain, hunger, homelessness, or being forgotten because of their age. We allow them to be free of medication, of strife, of rejection. We, as no others can, dearly love each of the souls represented here today."

The seven of them knelt and joined hands around the low table. They swayed rhythmically from side to side, as they sang a low, slow tune together.

Chapter Twenty-one

"MAMA, TO BE AS skinny as you are, you can cook like nobody's business." Lacey leaned back and patted her stomach. Her mother's spaghetti and meatballs, a recipe learned from an Italian roommate while in school, was so delicious. Lacey had, once again, stuffed herself with the meatless sauce base and tons of noodles.

Halloween spaghetti was a tradition at the Terry household. To this day, Lacey believed it came about as a ploy to get them home earlier from trick or treating. Also, to diminish the impact of Halloween. Her family understood that Lacey had never been keen on that holiday.

Her father chuckled. "If I didn't run three days a week, could you imagine what I'd weigh?"

"Yeah, but I don't cook this way all the time. During the week, when I'm working, you're pretty much on your own, Nathan Terry," Joy said. "You can't blame me for your weight or lack thereof."

Lacey laughed. "She's got you, Dad."

"Yeah, yeah. Hey, when is Lainie coming home? You always cook a lot of good stuff when she's home."

Joy rose and began clearing the table. Lacey rose to help. "She gets off around mid-November."

"Weird how much I miss the little brat," Lacey

mused.

"You wouldn't say that if she were here," Joy said in a singsongy voice.

Lacey laughed. "Probably true. So why didn't Nanna come tonight?"

"She's having dinner with a new friend," her mother said, as they rinsed plates and loaded the dishwasher. "It's this young woman she met at the library. Someone new to town." Joy rose from the dishwasher and dried her hands. "Her name is Sarah, and Mama says that she is just the most pitiful thing. She's been in a house fire, and she has scars all over her arms and face."

Lacey frowned. "Oh, that's so sad. Nanna always has had a soft spot for injured people."

Lacey's phone suddenly played "Bad Boys" from the reggae band Inner Circle.

She grimaced. "Excuse me, Mom, gotta get this."

"Another old guy," Sully said without preamble when she answered the phone.

Lacey took in a deep, shuddering breath. "This is getting crazy, Sully. Where?"

"It happened in some church downtown, but the body's already at Clevon's. Happened yesterday. The man's daughter let the firehouse take the body, because it was upsetting her kids."

"Does Clevon think it's natural?" She chewed on a thumbnail.

"Now, that I don't know. I told him I was calling you, and he said that was a good idea. That's all I know."

"What church was it?"

She could hear Sully leafing through his notepad. "The Abiding Love Gathering. It's that new one for the homeless. Opened next to where the Piggly Wiggly was. You remember that grocery store that closed downtown?"

Lacey nodded, then realized he couldn't see her. "Yeah. Where all those squatters are."

"That would be the place. Want me to meet you there?"

"No, Sully. You and Jimmy are on station duty tonight. And it's Halloween. I'll check it out."

"Okay, boss. Call if you need me."

She signed off and remained leaning against the hallway doorjamb for a long minute.

"Honey? Everything okay?" Nathan's voice brought her out of reverie. She turned slowly and faced him.

"We've got another death. Some old guy downtown."

"Oh no!" Joy exclaimed from the kitchen.

Lacey made her way back to the dining room. Nathan was still there, lingering over an after-dinner glass of wine. "Is it suspicious?" he asked, as she approached the table.

Joy came into the dining room as well. She was watching Lacey curiously. "Do you really think someone is murdering people in Queens Lot, Lace?"

"I don't know about suspicious, Dad. Just the fact that he is old, like the others, seems suspicious to me."

"Well, do you?" Joy interjected impatiently.

Lacey shook her head, feeling helpless. "I don't know, Mom. It sure seems that way. Something is going on and it's not natural. I am sure of that. We sent an alert out based on one guy who was seen by an eyewitness but haven't had any hits on it yet."

"Is that the one posted around town? That young man? I've never seen him before."

Lacey nodded. "You know, I did some research on serial killers. Kinda creepy, but I learned that they can look like anyone, like normal people. Heck, you could be one, Dad."

Nathan took on a deer in the headlights expression. "I don't think so," he stated in a huge stage whisper.

Lacey gave him a lopsided, indulgent smile. "You know what I mean. It could be anyone in town."

Joy shook her head. "I doubt that, Lace. We've known these people most of our lives. Why, all of a sudden, would someone start doing this? It has to be someone who moved here recently. I think you should focus on that demographic."

"I agree with you on that, Mom. It just seems like there's not that many new faces in town, you know?"

Joy resumed her seat at the table. "Some come in for the community college."

"I know, Mom." Lacey lifted her dark-blue uniform shirt from the back of her chair and pulled it on over her undershirt. "I guess I'd better scoot. I need to go downtown and check out the scene. It's in some new church for the homeless."

"Oh, Abiding Love. I know that church. Al—Atticus Weaver— used to work with me at the firm," Nathan said. "He started out running the front desk and ended up doing land deeds."

"And now he's a minister?" Joy asked.

Nathan chuckled. "Hey, I didn't drive him to it! He just got the call. He said he had to do something for all those people living on the streets downtown. He opened a church, and started a soup kitchen and a thrift store, all next to the rail yard."

Lacey smiled as she tucked in her shirt. "And

Queens Lot Financial had nothing to do with the startup, right?"

Nathan shrugged. "We might have helped a little."

"Umhmm." She leaned and kissed each parent on the cheek. "See you guys later."

"Lacey?" Her mother's low voice arrested her. "Be careful out there. We've never dealt with this kind of situation before in Queens Lot."

"Yes, expect the unexpected," her father added worriedly.

Lacey studied their dear, concerned faces for a long beat before nodding and heading out the front door.

Chapter Twenty-two

THE DOGS ALMOST KNOCKED Debra off her feet when she got home that evening. No doubt they had been made nervous by the few roaming trick or treaters that inevitably dropped by each Halloween.

"Damn! Take it easy, mutts!" she cried out as she shut the front door behind her.

She placed the two heavy bags she carried on the floor and led the dogs to the back door to let them out into the fenced yard. She moved through the living room, making sure the curtains were drawn and all the front lights were off. Tonight would not be a good night to be disturbed.

The house was oddly silent after the dogs were outside, and she realized anew how different the house was without her mother's nasty presence. But her mother was still there. She glanced toward the master bedroom doorway, as she moved back to fetch the things she'd purchased.

Using Halloween as an excuse, she had put both her two junior managers on duty, asking them to pass out candy to the little pagans. This allowed her to leave work early and, after checking in with Mother, she had driven all the way down into Washington County to an outdated hardware store in the center of a little town whose name she couldn't even remember. There she had bought the supplies she would need to do away with what was left of Mol. She had paid in cash and had then shredded the receipt with her fingers and given the shreds to the gentle fall breeze.

Her hands shook as she lifted the bags, but she carried them to the closed, master bathroom door and placed them on the floor. She pressed one palm to the wooden portal and smiled. She shook her head and frowned deliberately. Why was her mother's death such a source of amusement for her?

Angrily, she strode down the hall to her bedroom. Pulling her keys from her pocket, she suddenly realized that she never had to lock that door again. Awed and amazed by the thought, she slowly unlocked each deadbolt and threw the door wide. She went inside without closing it, even as she changed into a light pair of summer boxers and an old, casino T-shirt. She checked each computer and decided that the chat rooms could live a little longer without her.

Outside the master bath again, she took a deep breath and opened the door. A pungent odor hit her immediately, and she decided that her mother's bowels had evacuated. She'd read about that. She turned on the bathroom fan, glad that it was a quiet one.

Debra lifted the towel and looked down at her dead mother. Mol looked horrible. Most of the blood had begun to dry into a flaky-edged goo, and her mouth had stiffened in rigor mortis. The horrible grimace showed her large false teeth. Her eyes were open, but thankfully they were fixed with eerie stillness to the back of the bathtub. Her skin had become very white, and her hands had curled together in front of her chest.

Debra sighed in aggravation. Pissed that she had to get rid of her mother, having to tend to her yet even further, she jerked down the shower head and turned the water on. Warm. Mol's bowels and bladder had indeed let loose, and Debra diligently washed as much of it as she could down the drain. After turning off the water, she fetched the two bags from the bedroom then left the bathroom to fetch the five-gallon bucket she used when washing the car. It was kept ready in the laundry room, and she had to dump out sponges and bottles of cleaning solution.

She carried the bucket to the bathroom and placed it next to the tub. From one bag, she took out boxes of vinyl gloves and black garbage bags, an electric knife and a filleting knife. The other bag held the five containers of lye she had managed to find. Lye—sodium hydroxide—was hard to find these days and was somewhat regulated because of all the people using it to make methamphetamine. She had gotten one box of caustic soda from King's, where she worked, two boxes from the hardware store, and two bottles of drain cleaner from the convenience store near the little town. The bag also contained a pair of bright-blue, thick rubber gloves, necessary for dealing with the lye.

Using the filet knife, she ripped three holes in one of the garbage bags and pulled it over her head, making a type of protective apron. Next, she pulled on a pair of vinyl gloves and knelt next to the tub.

"So, here we are, Mol. Hell of a place to be," she said softly, as she used the sharp knife to slit Mol's slip. "Wish I could say you'd be missed, but truthfully, it'll be such a relief not to listen to your bullshit anymore."

She fell silent as she focused on cutting and pulling the slip from under her mother's stiff body. Managing to pull it loose, she shook open another trash bag and placed the blood-soaked slip inside. She tossed the scissors that she had used to kill Mol into the sink basin and bent back to her task. She sliced off the cotton panties Mol wore and disdainfully passed the urine and feces soaked garment into the bag as well.

"Man, you are foul," she whispered. "No surprise, that."

Debra was no surgeon, and it took her slightly longer than four hours to methodically slice all the flesh from her mother's bones and disarticulate the skeleton. Luckily, the knife had been new and super sharp. When finished, she expected it was more a useless piece of metal than a knife. Cartilage, sinew, and bony protuberances were not filet knife friendly. She had once been curious about how a body held together and this dissection had certainly satisfied that curiosity.

She dropped the knife next to the pile of bones in the bottom of the tub and sat back on her heels. Her shoulders, arms, and wrists screamed in anguished pain. The five-gallon bucket next to her was overflowing with flesh, and there was a pile of bloody, sinewy flesh still in the tub next to her mother's skull. A little creeped out, she had covered Mol's eyes with a washcloth when the body shifted and those blank eyes looked at her. She had even held the cloth in place while slicing the flesh from Mol's cheeks and neck.

She rose. "So, this is what it all comes down to. A fucking pile of bones and meat. Pretty boring if you ask me," she muttered. "I bet you never thought of that, did you, Mama? All that bellyachin' you done and for what? Bones. Meat." She kicked the bucket, causing the flesh and fat to wobble. One slice fell off and hit the tile floor with a solid, wet smack.

She leaned and turned on the shower head again and hosed down the tub once more. The washcloth on

Mol's skeletal face slipped and slid part of the way down. One milky eye glared at Debra and she giggled.

"Peepeye," she said, still giggling.

She left the bath and moved to the kitchen. The dogs whined to come in, so she opened the door absently as she searched for a large bowl. She finally located the wide, shallow bowl her mother had used for potato salad and took it with her back to the bathroom. The dogs followed at her heels, almost tripping her. When they got to the bathroom door they paused, noses in the air, twitching. Debra noticed and giggled.

"You babies are hungry, aren't you? Just wait, Debbie's got some nummy nums for you."

She quickly shut the door and the dogs whined in frustration. She moved back to the tub and began slicing the flesh into small chunks, using a folded hand towel as a cutting board so she wouldn't mar the side of the tub.

"Your puppies sure do love you, Mama. Sure do. Glad you'll be able to stay with them a while." She looked at the one expressionless eye and laughed helplessly.

Chapter Twenty-three

THE ABIDING LOVE BAPTIST Gathering building, the only active business in a defunct strip mall, appeared deserted when Lacey drove up. She radioed in to Sully, telling him that she had arrived, and then stepped out into the breezy evening. She adjusted her duty belt and walked to the storefront door of the church. She peered through the glass and saw a small group gathered inside, probably ten people. They were sitting without lights on, but it was early yet. They probably just hadn't needed them this soon. She opened the door and stepped inside, which caused all heads to swivel in her direction. She waved self-consciously.

Seconds later, a tall black man stepped away from the group and approached her, hand outstretched. She took the hand in greeting.

"Hello, Sheriff. I'm Reverend Al Weaver. Bad business today. Very bad business. Although, if it's time for the good Lord to take you, I can't think of a better place than in a sanctuary consecrated to Him."

"So, there was nothing...unusual about the death?" Lacey asked, studying him. He was handsome and charismatic. Being a preacher was probably a very good job for him.

"Oh, no, Ma'am. Here, come and sit with me." He indicated a nearby pew, and Lacey preceded him into it.

He settled next to her, shooting his cuffs and straightening his tie. "There was nothing unusual, that I could see. He sat on that pew there. I was up front, of course, so couldn't see but so much."

"Did you see anyone talking to him?"

He smiled and a short, low laugh escaped him. "We are a house of love, Sheriff. We begin every service with greeting and hugging our neighbor. It shows that we are all one, no matter our status in life, rich, poor, homeless, middle class. None of that matters in God's eyes, and I like to stress that at each service."

Lacey looked at the pew he indicated. "So, you're saying that he spoke to everyone on his row? Did you know the people sitting on either side of him?"

He shook his head and frowned. "No, I'm sorry to say I did not. This is a new church, and I am still learning the faces and names of my flock. I really can't remember anything about those sitting next to him."

They fell silent, and Lacey sighed. "How did you discover the deceased? If you don't mind me asking."

"Let's see. We were well into the service when Alisha Bowles realized that Ed had fallen asleep." He gestured one hand apologetically. "She told us this after the service was over, of course."

"Of course," Lacey agreed, nodding.

"Well, she said when the service was finished, she tried to wake him, because his daughter had come to pick him up. You probably know Kelly Reid? She teaches over at the high school."

Lacey screwed up her brow in confusion. "Is her dad homeless?"

The reverend shrugged. "She's opened her home to him, but he prefers his independence. And him on oxygen, no less. I think she was coming to get him to stay with her for a few days. It was quite a shock."

"I bet," Lacey agreed. "He was on oxygen, you say?"

"Yes, one of those little tanks."

"So, he just fell asleep and died? What did the fire department say when they got here? Did they say what they think caused it?"

The reverend spoke slowly, thoughtfully. "Nooo, they checked his lines and said oxygen was still flowing. We all assumed his heart just stopped."

Silence fell, each lost in private thought. Finally, the reverend cleared his throat. "Tell me, Sheriff. I take it that you are thinking our dear Edward might not have died a natural death?"

"I don't know. I just don't know."

He nodded. "Yet, you are investigating it as such?"

"Yes."

He shifted and sighed. "Well, I suppose I could ask around, quietly, to see if anyone else noticed anything."

Lacey watched him closely. "You'd do that?"

"Of course. Your father has always been very good to me. I would do anything to help you. Also, if someone has done something to Edward, he should be punished."

"By God?" Lacey asked.

"Of course. But God gives us laws to follow, as well. Romans tells us we should always obey the laws of man unless they conflict with the laws of God."

"I see," Lacey said, coming to her feet. "I guess I'd better let you get back to your group. Do you mind if I look around a bit before I leave?"

"Of course not." He took her hand in his and held it briefly. "We are having a private meeting up front so please ignore anything you might hear."

Lacey thought it an odd request, but as the lights were turned on and the meeting resumed, she quickly realized it was an Alcoholics Anonymous meeting. She smiled as she bent down to examine the pew where Edward had died. Seems like Reverend Weaver was truly doing good things for this poorly served community.

She spent several minutes studying the area but saw nothing significant. She walked around the middle of the church, ever spiraling toward the back of the sanctuary. She saw nothing notable and eventually left the building.

Outside, she studied the neighborhood surrounding the church. Downtown Queens Lot had once been centered around a railway station, a hub used for transporting cotton east during Queens Lot's heyday, back in the late eighteen hundreds. That was before the boll weevil infestation just about did away with the Lot's cotton industry. Today the rail lines had been abandoned. Not even travel trains came through, much less freight, and the homeless had taken over the rail yard.

Staring west, away from the gathering dusk, she saw several large metal cans on fire with people crowding around them. It wasn't that cold, really, but Lacey assumed that the centralized flames were comforting and provided a sense of unity. The homeless congregated here had made the graveled and concrete area a rather large tent city, but they kept it orderly. A fact she was grateful for. The idea of all these families living here dismayed Lacey, but she knew that with no real industry in town, there were just no jobs for these people. Queens Lot was a dying town. The young fled east to the bigger cities, while the middle-aged and elderly scraped by as best they could.

Lacey had been very lucky, able to work in her father's accounting firm before training to become a sheriff's deputy. Otherwise, she might have had to head east as well. A troubling thought, that. Wearily, she slid into the cruiser and pulled out onto Texan Street which would take her back to Hawthorne. She radioed Sully and told him she was heading home.

Chapter Twenty-four

"THANKS FOR MEETING ME," Lacey said to Bertie, as they slid into a scarred and carved up two-top at The Bean. It was early Tuesday, before work, and Queens Lot was slowly coming to life around them.

Bertie studied Lacey, noting her worried demeanor. "No problem, glad to get to see you. Everything okay?"

Lacey sighed. She gazed out the window as though diligently studying the Bob's Computer sign across the street. She lifted her coffee and took a healthy swallow.

"It's strange, you know? I worked so hard campaigning to get this job because I hated what Wade was up to. How he ran the office."

"Yep, I remember," Bertie replied, wondering where Lacey was going with this. Did she feel inadequate for the job? "And?"

Lacey abruptly changed topic. "Do you remember when you first came to town three, four years ago?"

Bertie smiled at the memory. "I do. And I remember how handsome you looked in your deputy uniform. I was applying for a teaching job at the school, wasn't I?"

Lacey nodded. "Yep, and I was there working the summer program for the kids. Some law info thing."

Bertie tilted her head to one side, eyes roving

across Lacey. "What did you think when you first saw me?"

Lacey laughed and sat back in her chair. "Oh man, what didn't I think? I thought you were adorable. And sexy. We mustn't forget sexy."

Bertie grimaced playfully. "I don't know about that. I have to ask...why are you remembering all this now?"

"I was trying to think about new people coming to town. Seeing if I could catch a break that way."

"Catch a break on what?" Bertie stirred a second packet of sugar into her coffee.

"These murders, you know, of all the old people." Lacey blinked slowly.

"Ahh," Bertie leaned back. "So, you do suspect murder. I wasn't sure what you had decided."

Lacey leaned forward eagerly. "Just look at the evidence! We've got like seven or eight people, older people, who have died in the space of a few months."

Bertie knew she had to be the reasonable one. "What? You're not serious. Queens Lot does have a lot of older people though. Maybe it's all natural. You know...like it just caught up with a handful of them all at once."

Lacey shook her head. "Nope. Gut says differently. As a cop, I have to trust my gut. It's too many bodies and they're like...posed. Like with respect."

"Respect?"

"You know, hands folded, the bodies laid out peacefully."

Bertie sighed. "Well, I guess that's a good thing, but suppose they all just died peacefully in their sleep? That does happen." She took a sip of her sweetened coffee.

"Naw, not like this." Lacey turned abruptly and

shouted through the empty café. "Hey, Ellen!"

Ellen DeMalley, the middle-aged owner of The Bean, poked her head out of the back office. "Yeah?"

"Don't you think it's weird how many old people are dying?"

Ellen rose and stepped out of her office. She approached the two women and took a seat next to them. "Hell, yeah. I seen more goddamned funerals this month than I have in the past ten years. Why you askin'?"

"She thinks we have a murderer in the Lot," Bertie answered for Lacey.

"A murderer?" Ellen screwed up her broad, freckled features. "Now, don't that beat all? Yeah, looks like you could say that, Sheriff. Sure has been a lot of people dying. Never had anything happen like that since old Gnat Knee Bennett plotted revenge and killed all those high school boys. I think that was back in sixty-eight."

Bertie leaned forward. She always liked a good murder story. "Why did he kill high school boys?"

Ellen smiled and crossed her arms. "Well, 'cause he was one hisself. Those boys picked on Gnat Knee from the get go. All his life, seems like."

"Why? What did he do to cause trouble?" Lacey asked curiously.

"Oh, he didn't do nothin', it's just 'cause he was so goddamned skinny! Wadn't an ounce of flesh on that boy. They started callin' him Gnat Knee when he was just a bitty thing, and his old, bony knobby knees poked out his trousers."

"Strange name, but I see how it came about. So, he was bullied pretty badly, huh?" Bertie asked.

"He was." Ellen fell silent and looked out the

window, watching storefronts across the street open for the day.

"So, what happened," Lacey prodded.

"Well, this went on all through school. I felt so damned bad for that boy. He had a rough time, getting beat up or lied about. Some say he was, uhm, molested in the showers. They just never gave him a moment's peace. Then, one day my friend, Maizie Nixon, slid on up to him at a basketball game and started talking to him. She told me later that she was just amazed by how smart he was and fun to talk to. He actually made her laugh out loud. So, they started keeping company. That didn't set well with the youngest Sims boy, Wallace, and he just lit in to old Gnat Knee with all he was worth." She paused and fell into reverie.

"The things they did to that boy. Half that we don't even know about. The worst was when Wally got Maizie alone and practically raped the poor gal. He didn't quite get there, thanks to him bein' interrupted, but he woulda if he coulda. She said she knew that for a fact. Well, when Gnat Knee got wind of this, he walked around for two days with smoke and fire practically coming out of his head."

"So, he was mad?" Bertie's gaze roved across Ellen's plump, friendly features.

"Mad ain't the word for it! The sheriff back then, old Porter Nash, told me that Gnat Knee quietly set about making his revenge. He went and set up traps for those boys who had bullied him so. Traps like wire stretched between two trees, bear traps, dangerous fireworks. Getting them when they least expected it. Well, his traps ended up *killing* five boys, including Wally. I'll never forget Maizie's face when Sheriff Nash came to take Gnat Knee away."

"That's downright horrible," Bertie exclaimed.

"Well, I certainly don't think these murders are due to revenge. I think that would be stretching it a bit too much," Lacey said.

Ellen nodded. "This seems like a lot different, doesn't it?"

Bertie picked up her mostly empty cup and sucked down the last few drops. "It looks to me like someone is trying to put old people out of their misery."

"Hey," Lacey snapped. "Who says they were miserable? Not all elderly people are sick or in pain. Some cultures even honor and cherish their elderly. Look at Japan, for example, or the Greek people. Native Americans. Old doesn't necessarily equate to ill and infirm, you know."

"Whoa!" Bertie loved it when Lacey got worked up. It made her even more beautiful. "I didn't mean to stir the bee's nest. It just could be what they're thinking if they are killing the elderly."

Lacey laughed and slumped back in her chair. "Sorry, Bert. This thing just has me sideways, is all."

Ellen stood and straightened the waistband of her jeans. "Good luck on that, Lacey. If I can do anything to help, now you just let me know, okay?"

Bertie stood and tossed her cup into the nearest bin. "That goes for me too, Lace. Seriously."

Lacey stood as well. "Thanks, guys. I'm heading over to Clevon's now to see what I can see about this latest body. Y'all keep your fingers crossed for me."

After saying their goodbyes, Ellen and Bertie watched through the large glass front as Lacey got into the cruiser.

"If anyone can get to the bottom of this, Lacey can," Ellen mused. "She's sharp as a tack."

And absolutely beautiful, Bertie thought. "Yep, I have no doubt of that," she said aloud, as her eyes caressed Lacey from afar.

Chapter Twenty-five

THE FOREVER REST FUNERAL Home was bustling with well-dressed people when Lacey arrived. She wondered why all the folks were gathered there and then she recognized Ronda Walls mother, Sue, weeping and supported by her family. Ronda's funeral was about to start. She made polite responses as she pressed through the townsfolk, until she finally saw Kasey and Bobby Cox standing together just outside the side entrance. She approached them.

"Hey, Bobby, hey, Kasey, do either of you know where Clevon is?"

"He's taking care of the Walls service," Bobby said. It was strange seeing him all dressed up. Kasey, too. Her usual attire was T-shirt and jeans, even when working front desk at the funeral home. "Are you here about Edward Jonas?"

Lacey nodded. "I am. Think Clevon would care if I go on down to see him?"

"Kasey will take you." He turned to his wife. "Can you get that report for her off my desk, hon?"

Kasey's smile was bright and breezy. "Sure. Come on this way, Sheriff."

The two made their way inside, delayed by a few more of the deceased's family members.

"Let me just pop in here," Kasey said. Lacey made

polite noises with Ronda's paternal grandfather, and then Kasey was back, leading her to the prep rooms downstairs.

"Wow, sure is quieter down here," Kasey said when they reached the studio that held Edward's body. He was indeed elderly, and his small, wizened form rested on the metal table, covered by a pale-green sheet. "I'll leave you to your exam," she said, handing Lacey a folder. "This is the report Clevon put together."

"Thanks, Kasey," Lacey said, and then a thought occurred. "Uh, Kasey? What do you think of Clevon?"

Kasey turned back from the doorway. "Um, Clevon? He's all right." She looked around nervously. "He's a little, you know, eccentric, I guess."

Lacey indicted Edward. "Do you think he does right by the bodies? I mean, he does a good job, right?"

Kasey screwed up her brow. "I...I think so. We never come in when he's doing the embalming, although he's taught Bobby how to do it and let him do one."

"Male or female? The one that Bobby did."

"Uhm, it was that man, Spence, I think." She looked hopefully toward the hallway, and Lacey could sense her discomfort.

"Thanks, Kasey." She indicated the folder. "I'll check this out."

After Kasey left, Lacey approached the table and looked down at the square face of the grizzled man of color who lay there. His features were weathered but still handsome in that rugged way some men have. But he was pale now, of course. She turned aside and opened the folder.

The toxicology screen had been negative, as expected. The body had no unusual markings, except for a military tattoo on his left forearm. Lacey checked and saw that he did have records from the VA hospital. She shook her head. *What our country does to the military*...she idly wondered if he'd actually seen war.

One glaring fact snared her attention and held on like a painful toothache. During his examination of the body, Clevon found a small puncture, maybe a needle puncture in the man's left thigh, high up. Also, he had officially postulated that the death could have been caused by an insulin injection.

Insulin! Lacey snapped her head up. *Could that be what was causing all the deaths? Injections of insulin?*

Lacey frowned intently, trying to recall a case she had read about while studying to be a deputy. There was a case, in England, if she remembered correctly, in which a husband, a doctor, had injected his wife with insulin, and then tried to say she committed suicide. He was convicted of her murder eventually, but it had been a hard case due to a lack of clear evidence. Insulin was a hormone that quickly metabolized in the body and there would be no trace of it upon autopsy. She turned back to the body and sighed. Fat lot of good, knowing the murder method if there was no one person to pin it on.

Setting the folder to one side, she lifted the sheet covering Edward's left leg and had a look at the puncture. It was so tiny that she had the devil's own time finding it. When she did, she was astonished that Clevon had spotted the teeny, tiny reddish mark. Doubt filled her. How could such a tiny mark have killed a man, albeit a sick man? It just bent the borders of logic. Yet, she knew that the human body was a unique chemical balance and anything that teetered that precious balance could be deadly.

She reared back and replaced the sheet. The murderer had to be close to this man in order to get a needle into his thigh. Thighs were usually one of the more protected areas of the body. Why hadn't the killer injected Edward in the arm? Or even the waist? It just didn't make a whole lot of sense.

Nothing about this case made any sense. Lacey's thoughts flew to the research she had done about serial killers. One thing they all had in common was charisma. That, or the ability to become invisible and move like a wraith through any normal community. That was probably the most frightening thing to her. To be looking for someone with the visage of a demon was one thing, but to look at your neighbor as a serial killer—that was really scary.

"So, Edward, wish you could talk, my friend. Was it another homeless person who did this to you? Is that how he moves through the Lot so easily?"

She thought of Maureen and Ronald and realized that they weren't the type of people to help the homeless, really. And she knew nothing about Talbot Spence. He was a stranger who just happened up on some bad luck. And what about Alicee and Ray? Their murders had been so different from the rest, being violent and bloody. She shook her head, mired in confusion and possibility.

The prep room began to weigh on her then, as did the dead body only inches from her. The skin of her scalp contracted and hair stood up on the back of her neck. She turned to the doorway just as her phone bleated into life. The jarring sound sent her heart racing and made her stomach contract until she almost vomited. Quickly, she fumbled the phone from her belt and silenced it. She glanced at the body, as if Edward had been disturbed by the harsh sound.

"Sheriff Terry," she whispered before checking the caller ID.

"Sheriff? Reverend Al Weaver here. Are you okay? You sound funny. Maybe I called at a—"

"No, no, I'm fine," she assured him, righting her voice. "No problem, Reverend. What can I do for you?"

"Well, you remember I said I was going to ask around for you, to see if anyone had seen someone sitting with Edward Jonas?"

Lacey murmured agreement.

"Seems like Carver Jack, one of our volunteers, did see someone. It was a stranger, someone he didn't know at least. She was a black woman with dark skin and just skinny as a rail, he said. Carver said he noticed her because she looked so hungry, and he had planned to approach her after the service to see if the food bank here at the church could do anything to help her. She was gone by then though. He says she must have slipped out during the final prayer."

"A woman? Really." Lacey chewed a thumbnail. She hadn't expected a woman, though she had entertained the idea. And a woman of color. "Did Carver say what she was wearing? Or notice anything else about her?"

She heard the reverend shift position. "Just that she was old fashioned looking. Wearing a long dress and a sort of shawl thing. Oh, he said her hair was really short. He assumed she was awfully malnourished and had been for some time."

Lacey sighed and edged closer to the doorway, glancing back at Edward who thankfully, never moved. "Listen, Reverend Al, I can't thank you enough for doing this for me. You and Carver have helped me in a big way. I'll never forget that, you hear?"

She could sense his smile. "Happy to help, Sheriff. I sure hope you find out who hurt this man. If I hear anything else, I'll call right away."

She signed off and stood just outside the door to the prep room, tapping her phone against her bottom lip. A woman. Edward had probably been killed by a woman serial killer. That would explain a lot.

Chapter Twenty-six

IT'S ABSOLUTELY BREATHTAKING," SARAH said, as she tilted her head to examine the painting more closely. "You really do have incredible talent."

"I like it, too," Nancy said. "Hey, would you like to come help me lug all this stuff down to the show in Mobile? It's in December, right before the holidays. Oh my gosh, that's less than a month away."

Sarah turned to Nancy and indicated her left hand, a hand that was scarred and twisted from a car accident caused by the foolish seventeen-year-old she had once been. "Not sure how much help I can be, but I will do my best."

Nancy smiled at her and wrapped one arm about her shoulder. "It's mostly for the company, you know. That's what I'm really after."

A twinge of guilt twisted in Sarah, low down in her solar plexus, but she ignored it. It was an easy task. All she needed to do was remember how her life had panned out before she'd met Mother. Regularly beaten by her stepfather, with no mercy, she had quickly become a habitual runaway from the age of twelve. For some odd reason, no matter how she pleaded with the small-town deputies, how loudly she explained her home life, they always sheepishly brought her back to the front door of that rundown clapboard house and to her parents. This always set off another round of senseless beatings. This vicious cycle went on and on, until Sarah felt murderous rage fill her if she was even in the same room with her bastard of a stepfather.

Reclining in her pigsty of a bedroom at night, she would dream of ways to make him pay. After all, it was up to her; the law simply was not on her side. She had once loved school, and had done well there, but that option soured after the bruises and split lips had caused accusations of rebellion and fighting from the guidance counselors. Guidance, shit. They had guided her right into a pit of never-ending despair and hatred.

The youth support system in that backwoods, southwestern corner of Oklahoma had failed young Sarah, daughter of Barbara Felton, a daughter who had never quite dealt properly with the mysterious hunting death of her real father. Or so they said.

Actually, her father was seldom in her thoughts. He had been a boorish man who mostly ignored her if he had a hot meal, a cold beer, and hunting buddies to share bullshit with. Which was okay with her. The two of them had absolutely no common ground anyway.

See, Sarah loved books and neither her parents nor any of her obnoxious siblings ever picked up a book. And Sarah read constantly, everything she could get her hands on, even though she was teased by friends and family for being such an absent-minded bookworm. One favorite reading topic was medical nonfiction—case histories, autopsy and forensic findings. Odd subjects for a teenage girl, but thankfully, those books had given her the wherewithal for the ultimate revenge.

Using her lunch money, Sarah had bought a lightweight pair of rubber dishwashing gloves at the store in downtown Halls. Several nights later, when the moon was high and she'd screwed up just enough courage, she crept silently out of her bedroom window with the gloves and some clippers she'd found behind an old shed in the field out back. Once outside the window, she used moonlight to guide her steps over to the huge clump of rosie laurel that bordered the back yard. Clipping only the lowest branches so no one would notice, she soon had a precious, lethal armload.

She doubted that anyone in the family even knew what the bushes were, much less what could be done with the leaves and twigs. But Sarah knew. After a solid month of painstaking, clumsy work with candles and purloined serving spoons, she had a perfect distillate. Then it was only a matter of time.

If anyone noted her new, placid acceptance of kitchen-based chores, chores she had once railed against, they never said. But soon, quicker than she had anticipated, the entire family began to fail. Her stepfather was first, of course, and it wasn't unusual for someone with his obvious weight issues to develop heart trouble. It was expected, actually, so his illness went mostly unremarked upon. It took him three weeks to die of heart failure, even though his wife and daughters dutifully brought him healthy, low-fat, doctor-approved food when he was hospitalized. Her mother went next, just fell down dead on the bedroom floor one day while making the bed. Most supposed it was an aneurism, like the doctor said, but others thought she'd just pined away from grief after losing yet another husband.

Sarah had left home the day after the funeral, leaving the house and car and everything about her past life to her older sister and her three younger siblings. It didn't matter to her what happened to them and, although Sarah had left their favorite casserole in the fridge, she never wondered if they'd eaten it.

She supposed the horrific car accident on a busy Dallas freeway two years later was some kind of punishment. But it had changed her life in ways unimaginable. *Call me Mother*, the nurse had whispered, as she laid wet gauze on Sarah's destroyed skin and stroked her aching head. She'd been enthralled by Mother and, though Sarah was unable to speak, the two shared so much with their gazes. They shared love and pain and a common, unbreakable bond.

Mother had, of course, looked different then, but nonetheless so beautiful to the wounded teenager in need of someone who actually, if they didn't *really* care, at least *seemed* to care for her. Sometimes that was enough.

"I'm looking forward to it," Sarah said, pulling Nancy close and returning as warm a smile as her disfigured face would allow.

She caught sight of the angel then, outside the studio window. It was only Corey today, but the two of them would be enough to send Nancy Amelie off on her brand-new adventure. They would help her be young again.

Chapter Twenty-seven

MOTHER LOVED THE QUIET and darkness of night. So much could happen during those hours. It was ripe with possibility. She sighed with contentment. These angels were working out tolerably well, even though Sheba had let herself lapse momentarily. Mother probably should have been more stern with her, and she did ponder whether the angel needed a few refresher sessions, but overall, she felt that all the angels were keeping the commandments. Their time in Queens Lot was progressing well, and she hoped they'd be able to stay there for a very long time. And they could, as long as they all continued to live by the commandments. Simple rules. She intertwined her fingers over her belly, as she idly went over them in her mind.

Choose wisely. Only the elderly or infirm would receive the angels' blessing.

Show respect. The beloved one must be accompanied on his or her journey, guided there by an angel, preferably more than one. The corporeal part must be left in peace and harmony with the environment.

Maintain silence. Those on the outside could never fathom or approve the angels' mission in life, therefore only other angels could know which blessings had been bestowed.

Be invisible. Angels are never seen, only felt for a short time.

Obey Mother's law. Mother was the supreme benevolent angel and must always be respected as such.

These thoughts resounding in her mind, she drifted off into a light, easy sleep. Several hours later, a scream ripped from her throat and she sat bolt upright in the bed, the light afghan she had covered the sheet with, flying to one side. Breath rasped in and out of her lungs, as she tried to pinpoint what had caused such a strong reaction and drawn her into immediate wakefulness.

She grimaced in concentration, suddenly feeling a dark, spiritual chasm open before her. She turned from side to side, alarmed and listening intently, as though psyche could be borne on sound. What was it? Gaining control of her breath, she quickly crossed alpha fingers which would allow her to fall into a very familiar trancelike state. She sent her own psyche out, pushing herself against the walls of reality. Nothing here, nothing here, nothing there.

Then she gasped as waves of information hit her. An awful truth inserted itself. Had an angel failed her? Had someone broken one of the commandments and chosen not to seek absolution by confessing their indiscretion to her? Mother leapt from the bed to stalk pensively about the room. She hated that it was happening again. Time after time, her paradigm was forced to shift.

If only there were some way to keep away the inevitable decay, but the visions of devolution were never specific enough to prevent trouble before it happened. Mother was an excellent projector, as evidenced by years and years of angel conversions, but she was not the best receiver. She often found the usually general information too muddied to decipher specifically. It was a frustrating nuisance, and the lack contributed to the entropy of their work.

Mother didn't want to leave Queens Lot. She felt comfortable here, almost accepted. She had wearied of the pressing mission, the gypsy lifestyle. Walking into a new town, setting up a new home, finding new angels among the city's forgotten and abused. Sometimes it felt too hard.

A new blast hit her. She sensed that an angel, a female angel, had betrayed her somehow. She gasped aloud and vomit rose high in her esophagus. She swallowed hard, fighting for control. Something very bad had happened, something that could put all of them in jeopardy.

She took stock of where each angel was at that moment. Corey was at his home in town, because he had to be at his courthouse job early the following day. Danny and Kenton were in their beds, in the house. She had tucked them in. The male angels were all accounted for.

Now the girls. Mother had bid Bathsheba goodnight as the angel had entered her cell-like bedroom. Sarah had been late returning to the house, because she had gone out of town for groceries. Had she come home yet? Could something have happened to her?

Then there was Debra, who had been oozing a troubled aura for at least a week. She was, supposedly, at home with her mother, but Mother couldn't get a read on her. So, which one had transgressed, Sarah or Debra? Which one would be the one to cause the Benevolent Mother to destroy yet another family of angels and force her to move on?

Anger rang through Mother and her face twisted in growing fury. The females were always problematic, harder to coerce and control. In each city, it seemed that the females always led to discovery and chaos.

She moved to the window and looked out at the sleeping town. "I really liked you," she told the slumbering residents sadly, softly.

She thought with regret about her new task, sending her angels on to their next journey. Some she would not miss, but Sarah and Corey had come to Queens Lot with her. Their accompaniment had been a new experiment, a trial to see if she could bypass fickle human nature and create a forever family, one that could travel the country with her, doing their charitable duty. If Sarah had failed her, then the experiment had failed and she would never try again.

A tear escaped one dark-brown eye and she swiped at it angrily. Damned small towns. Next time, she would go to a big city where people were more desperate and needy. Maybe she could find better loyalty there.

Chapter Twenty-eight

THE INDISTINGUISHABLE RURAL ROAD seemed as though it was going to go on forever as Debra drove into the deepening dusk. Darkened trees loomed menacingly large on each side of the road, making her feel claustrophobic. Finally, she spied the sign for the Crimson Yew Recreation Area and turned in.

This final resting place for her mother's remains was chosen because Debra knew about the abundance of wild boar in the area. There were so many boar along Yew Trail that hunters were often given license during proscribed times to hunt the beasties, receiving cash credit for each one they brought in. These boars were horrible creatures, just as likely to gore you or your child with their heavy tusks as to look at you. Brazen too, seeming to have no fear of the humans that periodically shared their lands. But, best of all, they were always hungry. This was what Debra was counting on.

"I think you'll like it up here, Mol," Debra said cheerfully, as she looked in the rear-view mirror. "Lots of trees, lots of animals. A good thing for you. Better than what you had before."

The two dark-blue buckets on the back seat gave no reply, but she continued on anyway. "And don't give me crap about bustin' up your bones. You know as well as anyone that it had to be done thataway. I can't be just laying your bones out here for anyone to find. I couldn't be sure that the hogs would eat it all, now could I?"

The contents of the buckets had soaked in lye for the better portion of a week, sloughing off what flesh Debra hadn't been able to carve from the bone. It also made the bones into lacy, brittle structures that she easily smashed into powder. Debra smiled at the mirror. She had almost enjoyed smashing her mother's brittle, faceless skull with a hammer. She sighed with dismay. Old wounds were the deepest, she supposed.

The asphalt road curved away from the deserted dirt trail that led left, and Debra dutifully followed that asphalt into the parking area. Head swiveling as she searched for security cameras, Debra hoisted both buckets from the back seat, once again surprised at how light her mother had become. A bucket in each hand, she kicked the door closed and hurried off into a wooded area to the right. She didn't want to go anywhere near the trail, because it was heavily used during the days, especially during the beautiful fall season. She didn't want anyone but the hogs disturbing dear old mom.

The going was rough, and her athletic shoes snared repeatedly on thick, half-buried roots, almost causing her to take a header each time. She found herself grunting like a pig herself, as she tried to hurry through the overgrowth, and she bit her bottom lip to force herself into silence. Dried leaves rustled with each step, however, and she had to force thoughts of snakes and ticks from her mind.

Soon, sweat sprouted on her brow and a strange nausea filled her. She had to stop, placing the buckets on the ground, to mop at her forehead with the hem of her T-shirt. Looking around, she had no idea where she was or how far she'd come. Everything looked the same. The forest around her was still, with not even a breeze stirring in the thick, fuzzy, vine-laden trees. Taking a deep breath, she lifted the buckets and headed off through the clearest path she could see.

She must have walked for another half an hour before she heard them. Wild boar. She smelled them too—a fetid, animal odor that made her nose wrinkle in automatic aversion.

"Guess this is it, Mama," she whispered, as she placed the buckets on a somewhat level piece of leaf laden ground. Quietly, she pulled the top off one and then the other. The last acrid smell she would have of her mother rose to greet her and the harshness made her turn her face away.

She lifted one bucket and let the wet mix of rough bone powder and decomposing flesh run out onto the ground. She tapped the bucket on the leafy ground to make sure all was out, then she recapped the bucket and set it aside. She turned the second bucket up the same way, strolling about a little to distribute the contents more widely. A harsh snort to her right made her aware of possible danger, so she quickly put the top back on the second bucket and grabbed them both to hurry back the way she'd come. She did pause to look back once and spied the huge lumbering shadows that were enjoying the last of her mother. The trek back to the parking lot and car was a nightmare. At least a half dozen times, she was sure she was lost and would be forever.

"Oh, Mother," she sighed, thinking of the one person who still truly loved her. How she wished she

were safe and sound at the old Lawrence house now.
Being there with Mother and the other angels would
make everything all right. Then she remembered that
she had secrets to hide from Mother, no matter how
much she wished she could tell her. No matter how
much she wished to confide in her and be comforted.

A strangled sob escaped Debra, and she pressed
her lips together as she trod heavily through the trees.
She remembered the first time she'd seen Mother.
Mother had *known* her. Mother had *seen*. Debra was
just a cashier at King's Stop & Shop then, but it hadn't
mattered. Mother, smiling at her in her checkout lane,
always made her feel special. She knew that was why
Mother had always chosen her line, because she, Debra,
was special. She had wondered, at first, if what they
had was some kind of lesbian love affair but quickly
realized that what Mother was offering was so much
more.

Debra's first attempt at taking a blessed one had
been a horrible experience. The wife walked in on the
taking of the chronically ill husband. And there was
blood. Debra hadn't understood that there should be no
blood, no violence. In her hurry to please Mother, she
had acted hastily, stupidly. But Mother had forgiven all.
They had talked again, extensively, about the gift of
passing and what it meant. She paused in her plodding
and stood still for a long beat. Yet another reason why
Mother must never know about Mol. Debra just could
not fail her again.

Chapter Twenty-nine

"HOW MUCH INSULIN WOULD it take to kill a man Edward's size?" Lacey leaned back in her chair, stretched out her legs, and crossed her ankles. She stared at her shiny black shoes.

Clevon snorted at the other end of the phone line. "Christ, Lacey. I don't know. It depends on how their body processes it...I'm still not sold on this murder theory of yours. These people dying are old and sick. Like I said, maybe it's just their time."

Lacey leaned forward and fiddled with the pencil cup on her desk. "I told you, I've got a gut feeling about this. Besides, you're the one who said it was an insulin injection."

"I said probable insulin injection. I'm not one hundred percent sure that mark isn't something he did to himself by accident or maybe an insect sting."

"With no swelling? I don't think—"

"Look, my other phone is ringing. Just file what I said. At least it wasn't a ruling of inconclusive this time. Good luck trying to investigate it."

Lacey was abruptly listening to dead air. "Hell and damnation," she shouted.

"You all right, boss?" Frank stuck his head around

the door jamb, peering into her office.

"Yeah. Just dealing with idiots," she replied sullenly.

Frank laughed and smoothed his hand across his dyed, jet-black hair. "Same shit, different day."

Lacey nodded. "You got that right. Hey, did you take that drawing around?"

Based on Carver Jack's recall, Frances had sketched a picture of the church woman, and Frank had been asked to take it around to the homeless area downtown to see if anyone knew her.

Frank stepped completely into the room. "Sure did, but it was a wash. No one even said they'd seen her 'cept one rummy who swore he saw her praying and beating at herself out behind the Dollar Barn a few months ago. Said her prayin' woke him from a sound sleep."

Lacey grunted. "You believe him?"

Frank shrugged. "Who the fuck knows? He coulda dreamed it, but he swore on his mama's grave."

"And he would sleep in that alley a lot," Lacey added thoughtfully. She wondered if religion could possibly have something to do with the deaths.

"Will you do a check and see if any of the victims have a church or a club or a religious affiliation for me?"

He pursed his lips before speaking. "Absolutely, but I think we're grasping at straws here, Sheriff. A woman would just have to be bat-shit crazy to go around killing old people."

"That's why I wanna look into a religious connection. Makes perfect sense, doesn't it?" She watched his face closely, and it took him about half a minute to get her comment and become offended.

He waved an oversized hand at her and his blue

eyes narrowed. "Now, Sheriff, ain't no call to be—"

Lacey interrupted him hastily. "Come on Frank, you know I was pulling your leg. I do agree with you. Seems like we have a true crazy person running loose around the Lot."

Frank made a face of tolerant understanding. "I'll get right on it, boss."

After Frank left, Lacey turned to the blotter clipboard and saw that life in Queen's Lot was going on as usual—a little graffiti, a little theft, a little speeding, a few drug possessions. She cradled her forehead in both palms. How she wished she could unknow what she knew in her gut. How she wished that Clevon and just about everyone else she talked to would be right. That all these unexplained deaths were from old age or illness. It would make her life so much easier.

"Lacey?"

Lacey lifted her eyes and saw that Erva stood in the office doorway. She looked as though she'd seen a ghost, her face ashen and grim. "Yeah?"

"Your dad just called, and he wants you to come out to your Nanna's house right away."

Lacey's heart missed a beat, and she stood shakily. "Why? What's happened?"

Erva's eyes were filled with pain. "Just go, hon, go on. Sully's waiting in the cruiser." She took Lacey firmly by the bicep and rapidly propelled her toward the outer door. "Don't worry about a thing here. Just go be with your family."

Lacey remained silent and numb during the short ride to her grandmother's house, and her heart sank low in her chest as she saw Clevon's van parked in the tree-shaded driveway. A low moan escaped her, as she stepped from the cruiser. She knew what she would find, and she tried to swallow that knowledge, to take it in and moderate it until she could get a handle on the pain.

Sully was suddenly there next to her, and he took her arm in support. "Steady on, Sheriff, steady on," he muttered.

She was grateful for his strength, but there was a huge part of her that just couldn't go inside. Her legs wouldn't move. There was no way she could enter that dear, beloved house and see what she knew she would find there. Sully waited patiently, as Lacey lifted her eyes and studied Nanna's studio on the left, its add-on brick incongruous but working somehow. She looked to the right, to the front porch, and saw her father waiting for her, one arm braced high against a white pillar, his face buried in his bicep. The bright, yellow cushions on the seats behind him were a huge contrast to his grief, lying to all of them with their cheerfulness.

"I don't think..." Lacey began but bit her tongue to hold back her admission of weakness. She had to go in. She had to make sure that she did right by her grandmother. Suddenly, she realized she had to know what had happened to her beloved nanna. She was the sheriff, and she had to do her job, which was to determine whether a death was suspicious in nature.

"Come on, Lacey," Sully murmured, as if reading her thoughts.

Implementing one of the hardest actions of her life to date, Lacey freed a foot from the ground beneath her and moved it forward. Leaning heavily on Sully, her forearm snaked around his, she pulled another foot forward. Thus they made the trek to the porch, a trek that could have lasted an hour or a minute. Lacey was digging deep, mustering every bit of courage in her being.

"Oh, Lace," her father said in a low, breathy voice. "I am so, so sorry. I know what she meant to you."

Lacey allowed her father to transfer her grip from Sully to his own forearm and lead her inside. She breathed in the familiar orange scent characteristic to Nanna's house, and tears welled in her eyes. The future seemed a grim, grim place without her nanna.

They took a sharp left and stepped through the dining room and into her grandmother's studio. Lacey didn't see her at first, but then a scrap of bright-yellow shirt caught her eye. Pulling free from her father, Lacey brushed past Clevon and Billy and knelt next to the hideous flowered sofa where her beloved nanna lay. She looked peaceful, actually asleep, with her hands folded one atop the other. Her head rested to one side, and her white hair was not even mussed.

"What happened, Clevon?" Lacey asked, her voice gravelly with grief and growing anger.

"Now, Lacey...." Clevon began, spreading his hands wide.

"Nathan?" The worried voice of Lacey's mother sounded from the open front door, echoing throughout the now cavernous house.

A flurry of motion behind Lacey implied that her father had gone to break the news to his wife. This was proven by the wails of anguish that sounded next. Lacey could not be involved in comforting her mother. All she could do was smooth the short hair back from her grandmother's forehead. "Ah, Nanna," she muttered sorrowfully, repeatedly, as though in reprimand. "Ah, Nanna."

Her mother appeared suddenly next to her. Lacey turned to her, noticing that the gathered men had

stepped back to give the two women—and Nanna—
their space. Joy pulled Lacey into a strong, binding hug.
Lacey could cry then and she did. Weeping and wailing,
the two women clung together in their loss.

Chapter Thirty

"LACEY, YOU REALLY AREN'T supposed to be here. You are a family member, after all," Clevon said, as he untied and removed Nanna's shoes.

Lacey studied Clevon with dull, angry eyes. "I'm also the fucking sheriff of this goddamned town, and I am investigating a suspicious death. So, don't you be telling me what I can or cannot do, Clevon Stringer."

Clevon raised his head and squinted at her, one of Nanna's white sneakers still held in his hand. "Don't you be taking on airs with me, girl. I'm just telling you what the law book says." He paused, studying her. "Look, I know you're hurting. I understand how hard this must be, just...just don't take it out on me, okay?"

Lacey nodded that she'd heard him, but her tone was dismissive. "Just get on with it, Clevon."

He sighed and shrugged. "Whatever you say, Sheriff."

Sitting on an empty autopsy table on the opposite side of the body, Lacey's stomach was twisted into one hard knot. When she thought about that, it became very hard to breathe. So, she didn't think about it. She also didn't think about the fact that the corpse on Clevon's other metal table was her beautiful grandmother. She couldn't think about that. She was, nevertheless, filled with a keen protectiveness concerning this body. She knew she had to be with this body during every aspect of the autopsy and preparation.

Clevon lifted scissors from a nearby counter and methodically began slicing the body's knit trousers and bright-yellow shirt vertically along the front. He glanced at Lacey before pulling a pale-green sheet from a drawer. He snapped it open and it wafted gently down to cover the body. Reaching under, to protect the body's modesty, he gently pulled the clothing out from under the sheet. He folded the sheet toward Lacey's side of the room, bunching it somewhat, as he quickly cut away the underthings. He pulled the sheet forward again and fetched a basin and cloth from the sink.

"Better look away for just a minute, Lacey. I'm going to examine her for marks while I wash her," he told her as he filled the basin with water from the springy faucet overhead.

Lacey sighed but dutifully turned her head to one side and let her mind wander, as she purposefully thought of nothing beyond the sound of running water. She eventually pulled out her cell phone, but the notifications were all condolences from the townspeople she served. She couldn't deal with that quite yet. She thought about her mother, led away by her dad, her face blank and disbelieving. It was funny how none of them had prepared for this day. It was as though they were all certain Nanna's light would never dim.

Lacey swallowed a sob and turned back to see the wet, covered body lifted to one side, as Clevon studied the back, the bottom, and the legs. She tore her gaze away when she saw the torsion in the neck as the head hung to one side. She covered her eyes with her hands, fighting the urge to retch again. She had already emptied her stomach before getting back into the cruiser, and the bile had lain heavy in the back of her mouth as she and Sully followed the Forever Rest van back to the funeral home. She wouldn't be sick, she wouldn't be sick.

"Okay, Lacey, I don't see anything. No needle punctures, no cuts or bruises," Clevon said some time later, his voice shattering her pervasive mantra about not being sick.

Lacey dropped her hands and ceased rocking to and fro, an action she wasn't even aware she was doing. She looked at the medical examiner. "So. What killed her?"

He leaned and studied the body's face, his fingers lifting her eyelids. He rose up. "I'm thinking it's a natural death, Lacey. She was in her eighties."

Lacey was having none of it. "Are her pupils small?" she ground out, her voice sounding like iron filings even to her own ears. "Are her muscles lax?"

Clevon hung his head, and spreading both palms, laid them on the metal table, leaning his weight on his arms. "You just won't give up on this, will you?" he asked wearily.

She just stared at him, her gaze as fierce as she could make it.

He raised his head and looked at her. "Yes. Are you happy now? Your grandmother is probably a victim of the Queens Lot Serial Killer."

Lacey's eyes opened wide. "You prick! Am I happy now? You gotta be kidding me! I guess you've forgotten I carry a gun?"

A brief few seconds of alarm swept across Clevon's features, but then he frowned. "Calm down, Lacey. I didn't mean nothing by it."

Lacey gave him a look of pure disgust. "Just do the fucking autopsy and don't talk to me anymore right now. I've had just about all I can take today."

Clevon nodded and bent to the task of autopsy. Lacey, although it was extremely hard to stay during the process, knew she had to stay. One, because she owed it to Nanna and secondly, she wasn't sure she trusted Clevon alone with her grandmother. Thankfully, he was very cognizant of Lacey's continued presence. He worked hard to maintain Nanna's modesty and dignity, not an easy task when essentially tearing her apart and putting her back together again. By the time he'd finished, Lacey was filled with a type of exhaustion she'd never encountered before.

The coppery taste of blood filled her mouth, and she realized she had somehow caught her tongue between her clenched teeth. She forced her entire body to unclench, but she waited until Clevon had put the body on a stretcher and rolled it into a refrigerated room before she got up to leave. She even waited for Clevon to clean the room so that he could go upstairs with her. He walked her to the front door and waved his notes at her.

"I'll get these entered in and get it to you tomorrow, later today at the earliest," he said kindly.

Lacey took a deep breath and turned to face him as he stood in the doorway. "I'm sorry about earlier," she said haltingly.

He nodded and then turned away. "It's forgotten, Sheriff."

Chapter Thirty-one

SULLY HAD BEEN THOUGHTFUL enough to leave her the cruiser, no doubt calling Erva or one of the others to come get him. This was a very good thing, because Lacey had no immediate plans to return to the sheriff's department and her quiet, too reflective office.

Switching on the car, she sat idle a moment, seeking some type of peace. There was none forthcoming, so she let the car roll forward slowly. At the end of the Forever Rest parking lot, where it met Hawthorne, she gripped the wheel in indecision. She eventually decided to head east into town. At least then she could stave off some guilt with a small semblance of work by patrolling. What she really wanted to do was find a big, green field with a huge, green tree. She would sit under that tree and let loose all the rage, pain, and frustration she was feeling.

She passed Ryan Nash School and almost stopped to seek sympathy from Bertie, but she gritted her teeth and rolled on. She realized suddenly that in a town full of people she had known most of her life, she had no one, no real friend who would *be* there for her during a time like this. She shook off the self-pity, knowing that it was mostly her fault. Growing up gay in a small town meant she had to be constantly on guard, afraid that someone would guess her secret and that she would be shunned. Perhaps, this was why she had been more cautious than most during her high school years.

She often saw other women, straight women, with their close besties, going to the mall, attending baby showers and endless weddings, and church socials. Most of the time, she didn't feel the lack, but during times like this, times when she was sad, it would have been nice to have someone's shoulder to cry on. Someone besides her grieving mother.

She passed the pharmacy and the medical complex, the rail yard, then the courthouse. She passed the burger joint, King's grocery store, and the discount dollar store, but she didn't really see any of it. One thought penetrated and drowned out any present reality—there was no more Nanna in her world.

She shut her eyes, filled with unmeasurable pain. When she opened them, she was alarmed to see that someone had walked right out in front of her car. The woman stared at her in alarm, eyes huge, as Lacey slammed on the brakes, skidding the car onto the wide shoulder of the road, missing the woman by inches.

A profound silence fell after the gravel had settled. Lacey breathed in harsh gasps, one hand on her chest, as she tried to calm her racing heart. She knew she was seconds from keeling over from a heart attack, but she also knew she had to see if the woman was okay. She opened the door latch with one shaking hand and the door swung wide, creaking the entire way.

"Omigod! Omigod! Are you okay, Sheriff?" Dark, kohl-rimmed eyes peered at her through the door opening. "I coulda swore you saw me."

Lacey squinted up through the settling dust cloud. "Oh God, Sloane! I almost sent you right on to heaven. What in the world were you doing in the road?"

Sloane knelt, the pale skin of one knee showing

through her torn leggings. She studied Lacey. "Well, I wasn't really. You were driving kind of all over and kinda slow, like you were looking for something. I wanted to cross, so I waved at you. I thought you saw me 'cause you slowed down, but then you speeded up again. Are you okay?"

Was she okay? Good question. She sighed before answering. "Now, that's the question of the day, isn't it?"

Sloane's face grew kind in empathy. "Something happen, Sheriff?"

It took a minute, but Lacey was finally able to say it. "My grandmother was killed."

Sloane sat back on her heels, palms on her knees. "Killed? What? How did that happen?"

Silence surrounded them for a long beat, and finally Sloane stood and came around to the passenger side. She tugged on the locked door until Lacey pressed the release switch.

"Now, talk to me," she said, settling into the passenger seat and turning so that she faced Lacey.

Lacey turned and studied Sloane. Being of the Goth persuasion, Sloane wore black lipstick and heavy, black eyeliner, but her pale skin was smooth and seemed to glow behind the makeup. Her hair was short and spiky around the thick, upswept bangs, but the rest was long and ebony black. It looked silky, and Lacey had a sudden, crazy urge to run her fingers through it. Sloane was regarding her with eyes of the deepest brown, and she finally extended one ring-laden hand and laid it atop Lacey's right hand.

"I know how much you loved your grandmother."

Lacey could only nod, because her grieving heart had crawled up and settled somewhere in her throat. A car passed and the sound of it brought her back to full awareness. Lacey leaned to swing the heavy driver's side door closed. Again, there was silence.

"Where were you going?" Lacey asked, finally finding her voice.

"Just home. I finished my shift, so was heading home." She pointed down a side road that began on the other side of the road. Clementine Lane.

"Pretty name," Lacey whispered.

"Huh? What's that, Sheriff?"

"Nothing. Your road has a pretty name, is all." She reached for the key still in the ignition. "Let's get you home, now that I've almost run you over."

Slone nodded and buckled her seatbelt.

The shoulder was level, so Lacey was able to turn the car back onto the paved road easily. She guided it down Clementine, and after about a mile, Sloane indicated a small cottage set close to the road.

"This is me," she said.

The older home was pretty nondescript on the outside, but the tiny yard was well-maintained and flowers were planted on either side of the door. Lacey pulled in the narrow parking area.

Sloane thanked her and got out, then leaned in the passenger door opening. "Sheriff, you look like you need a drink. Why don't you come in and sit for a spell?"

Lacey looked behind her, back in the direction of town, and realized that she didn't, at this moment, care one iota what was going on back there.

"You know, Sloane, I might just take you up on that." She switched off the ignition and stepped from the car.

Chapter Thirty-two

"YES, HYRAM, YES. GO to the boy's room, but don't dillydally," Bertie said, finally acquiescing to the boy's persistent squirming. He rose and rushed from the room.

The rest of the class tittered, probably because she had used the word dillydally, but she didn't care. Her thoughts today were on her friend, Lacey, and how she was handling her grandmother's death.

"All right, we need to do this worksheet now, and I want you to pay special attention to question fourteen. That's the Atlantic Ocean, not the Pacific. You guys confused that one last time. Gotta know your oceans, kiddos."

Bertie walked along the two aisles, handing out the geography worksheet, then took a seat at her large and inevitably cluttered wooden desk. The creak of the classroom door drew her attention, and she smiled as Hyram took his seat.

"Good job, young man. Now, you all have half an hour to complete the worksheet. And please, no talking until the time is up. Start...now!"

She switched on her phone's timer, then watched with satisfaction as if one unit, they bowed their heads diligently over their task.

Her kids were good. She had no complaints. It was

weird having so many very young charges under her care. In the past, she had focused more on young adults more than fourth graders, so this was a nice change. She also was fortunate enough to get one of the best classrooms, lined with large windows on one side and lots of wall space on the other. Good for displaying educational materials. It had a large worktable area, as well, and wasn't as cramped as some of the older students' classrooms.

She turned and set her gaze outside the large bay window near her desk. Her thoughts flew back to Lacey and anger filled her. Nancy Amelie's death had been a shock and so senseless. She knew how destroyed Lacey had to be by her death. Bertie had sent a text message right away and later sent flowers to the Terry residence, but she wasn't sure what else she could do. She needed to see Lacey, but her calls had gone unanswered and this worried her. The vague idea that Lacey might go over the edge and hurt herself carped at the back of Bertie's mind. She didn't want to believe such a thing, but she knew something about Lacey's frustration with small-town life.

How she wished that she and Lacey could have remained together, been a real couple. She wondered if Lacey would go away with her. Maybe to a bigger city, such as Birmingham or even farther north, New York or Washington DC. After all, Bertie could teach anywhere, do anything, and Lacey could....well, Lacey would have to be a beat cop, probably, not a sheriff like she was now. Would she go for that? To be with Bertie? To be in a relationship?

Bertie sighed and pushed thoughts of Lacey from her mind. She glanced across the rows of students and felt warmth fill her. She so loved children. They were truly the hope for the future, the gauge of possibility, of what could be. She'd heard a quote once; she was not sure who first said it, but it always resonated with her—'youth lives on hope and old age on memories.'

Bertie was living more on memories than on hope now, and that saddened her. She could feel the aging process a little more with each passing year. She wondered idly about when the cutoff year was to be considered middle-aged. Was it fifty? Most healthy people could live to be almost one hundred nowadays. She didn't think she'd make it that far, so maybe for her it was where she currently was, her mid-thirties.

The alarm on her phone buzzed and Bertie stood. "All right, boys and girls. Please pass your worksheets to the front of the room."

She waited, and then gathered the worksheets from each front row desk. "Now, since Thanksgiving is coming, I think we should pay attention to all the wonderful things we are thankful for. For our writing exercise for today, we are going to move to the art tables and make a small booklet of all the things we are grateful for in our lives."

As she ushered the children toward the round tables on the other side of the room, her thoughts returned once more to Lacey, and she knew she had to seek her out. She needed to comfort her.

Chapter Thirty-three

SLOANE'S HOUSE WAS SLIGHTLY bohemian, hippie-like, making Lacey feel like she'd stepped into a time warp of some kind. It was so relaxed and peaceful that she felt immediately at home.

"Here." Sloane handed Lacey a glass of iced tea. "Come into the living room and sit down."

Lacey followed obediently, the cold glass chilling her fingers. The entrance of the house led, oddly enough, into a large open kitchen and dining area. The wooden dining table they passed on the way to the sitting area was substantial and attractive, but it was what was on top that captured Lacey's attention—bars of soap. Wrapped bars of Ivory soap were laid in a tidy semicircle around the back of the oval table, four bars high. There was also a large collection of decorative soaps in many different colors, even some of the lovely homemade bars made by Clancy Myers, who sold them at the florist shop.

Lacey noted the work area in the front center of the table. On top of several thick, rubber mats lay a strange, short-bladed knife, a stack of curly soap shavings, plus a handful of other metal and plastic tools.

"I thought I smelled soap when we came in." Lacey studied the carvings scattered across the table. "Do you do these?"

Sloane rushed toward the table as if embarrassed. "Um, yeah, I do. It was an old habit I picked up from my Grammy Williams. You remember her?" Sloane lifted the short-bladed knife and swung it nervously in her hands.

"What's this one? A turtle? And that, what's that?" Lacey leaned to snare a large four-inch square of handmade soap bearing a beautiful pastoral scene. "Is this...is this Japanese art?" She studied the incredible detail of the piece and traced one line with a finger. "How did you...?"

Sloane set the knife down. "It's like a transfer. You know, I find a picture I like, then I lay it on the soap and make holes in the picture for where stuff is gonna go. Then I...well, I kinda eyeball it and just make it look like the picture."

"Wow, that's amazing!" She lifted her eyes and studied Sloane with new appreciation. This river ran a lot deeper than anyone thought.

Sloane shrugged. "It's fun. I mean, there's not too many things to do in the Lot, so seems like a hobby is a good idea."

She pointed to one side. A shallow, wooden bowl lay filled with beautiful pastel-pink roses, both budding and in full bloom. She grinned as though embarrassed and sharing a great weakness. "These are my favorites. I just love doing them."

Lacey touched one of the buttery blooms, and found it to be smooth like the finest silk. "How do you get it so—"

"Smooth? I keep a bowl of water next to the sink just for this. I just smooth it in the water, wearing it away until it's just right."

Lacey's thoughts flew to her grandmother's similar

artistic sentiments, and sudden sadness washed across her again. Sloane must have sensed the renewed grief, for she studied Lacey with some compassion and then pulled her into a tight hug, not an easy task since Lacey was still in uniform and wearing her hefty duty belt and gun. It worked, however, calming her. And it felt really nice. Comforting.

Momentarily surprised, Lacey nevertheless pulled Sloane close, enjoying the sensation of the young woman's body against hers. Sloane often wore baggy, shift-type dresses or loose-fitting button-down shirts over leggings, so Lacey was surprised at how curvy she was despite her thinness. Sloane smoothed Lacey's back, and Lacey felt tears well. The hug lasted a long time before Sloane stepped back.

"Don't forget your tea," Sloane said, as she stepped into the living room.

Lacey swiped at her eyes, fetched her glass of tea from the table, and took a seat in one of the two recliners in the sparsely furnished television room.

"So, tell me about your grandmother," Sloane suggested gently. "And then I will tell you about mine."

The two talked long into the evening, and Lacey admired Sloane more with each sentence they shared. Sloane was a true pragmatist, very practical and very Zen-like in her outlook. Lacey was fascinated by the woman and marveled at how they had never connected before. Then something Sloane said made her remember that Sloane had come to Queens Lot to live with her grandmother after her mother died and her father disappeared. This was why Lacey never remembered her from school. Plus, she had been a year behind Lacey. Finally, something of a silence fell between them.

"Feeling a little better?" Sloane asked.

Lacey thought about it. Yes, she did feel better. Sharing her grandmother with someone who cared had been what she needed on this tragic day.

"Yes. Thank you, Sloane. You've really made a difference."

Sloane smiled and reached across to take Lacey's hand. "Wow. No one talks like that anymore, do they? You know, that someone made a difference. I think it's cool, though."

Lacey found that she was viscerally affected by Sloane's touch, and when Sloane's thumb moved sensually across the back of her hand, she lifted her eyes and watched Sloane quizzically.

Sloane, blushing, let go of the hand and sat back.

"Sorry, Lacey. I forget sometimes that everyone isn't like me."

"What do you mean?" Lacey asked when she could find her voice.

"Well, see, I don't think loving women is a bad thing just because I'm a woman. Not at all. I see it as positive, actually, maybe because my mother did. She was one of the most open-minded people I've ever met. I grew up with lesbians, even though my mother was straight, so it just seemed...normal to me when I realized I was gay."

Lacey felt shell-shocked by this revelation and also pleased. This was the way she would feel about her lesbianism if other belief systems wouldn't interfere.

"Wait. You said I'm not like you. But what if I am?"

Sloane slitted her eyes and looked sideways at Lacey. "I wondered. I have pretty good gaydar. You don't have anyone though?"

Lacey grunted. "In this town? You've got to be

kidding."

Sloane studied her in that quiet, piercing way she had. "You need to branch farther out. I made some awesome friends in Chatom, nurses at Southie Central. They've fixed me up with a few dates, but they never panned out to much. Call me a snob, but I like people who think, you know?"

"I do know." Lacey couldn't help the broad grin growing on her face. At last, someone she could be honest and open with. Someone who she understood and who might just understand her.

"Have you been dating at all?" Sloane asked, tilting her head in curiosity.

"A little," Lacey said on a sighing breath. "I had one gal I was with for a few months. I thought that might be for good."

"So, what happened?"

"The closet."

"Ahh, the closet." Sloane laughed lightly. "I burned my closet a long time ago. Seems to me, it's up to us to decide who makes the rules we live our life by. I chose, and still choose, me."

Lacey liked this.

"Hey, Sloane, want to go out with me?"

Sloane studied Lacey for a long beat. "You do know that you're the sheriff here, right?"

Lacey laughed. "Yeah, I know. But, it seems to me that maybe other things are just as important. So, dinner?"

"Do you like soap? It's a deal breaker." She waited, eyes amused.

"I love soap," Lacey gushed, laughing.

Sloane rose and moved to Lacey's chair. She stood in front of Lacey then bent down and brought their faces very close. "One kiss and then you go, okay?"

She pressed her lips to Lacey's, and Lacey felt something soar inside her. Sloane laid a palm against each of Lacey's cheeks and kissed each corner of her mouth and then the tip of her nose.

"There," she said, standing. "Our first kiss. How was it?"

Lacey had the devil's own time finding her voice. "Good," she finally ground out. "Very good."

Chapter Thirty-four

DEBRA HAD WAITED TOO long to take out the money from Nancy Amelie's account and now the account had been closed by a diligent family member. Mother could only stare at her with an astonished expression when she admitted the lapse. It was so uncharacteristic to find Mother bewildered that Debra fought the urge to laugh. This urge was counterbalanced by the horror she felt at letting Mother down.

"I didn't check my phone, so I didn't know she'd been sent on," Debra explained.

"It was two days ago, Angel. Where have you been?" Mother's voice was full of reprimand.

Debra sighed. Where had she been? Working, of course. *And getting rid of my fucking mother's body*, she wanted to scream. That was all she'd been up to, that was all.

Debra mumbled something incomprehensible, and then realized that Mother was examining her a bit too closely. "It's fine, I'm fine," she protested lamely. "I'm really sorry."

She felt nauseated suddenly, and realized that she was standing too close to Sarah's lab. The smells coming from there were horrendous. "Whew," she said, waving a hand in front of her nose. "That stuff she cooks up in there really stinks, doesn't it?"

Mother had tilted her head to one side, and she was watching Debra with that piercing, accusatory glare she could do so well. Debra felt a bubble of merriment rise in her again, and she tried once more to squelch it down. By doing so, she really wasn't able to speak very well. She looked away.

"Angel. I sense that something is wrong." Mother took Debra by the chin and forced their eyes to meet. Debra felt the old magic feelings that had once been there, but the thing growing inside her psyche had dulled it. She no longer felt like one of the Angel family.

"But I can still do it," she muttered.

"Do what, Angel?" Mother's gaze was full of concern.

"Why, what I need to do, of course. Take the money, take the beloved. I can do these things."

Corey, who had been reclined in an easy chair reading a magazine, suddenly rose up and stood behind Mother, his mien one of curiosity. "Mother? Everything okay?"

Mother waved one hand at him. "Shh, sure, Angel. All is well."

She turned her gaze back to Debra, who giggled nervously.

"Yeah, Cor-ey!" Debra said sarcastically. Mother's golden boy, always with his nose in everything. "All is well."

Debra pulled away from Mother's hand, and she saw Mother's mouth tighten into a grim line.

"Hey, don't give me crap," Corey said, stepping forward. "You're the one who fucked up. You know, we depend on that money to live. Depend on that money so we can continue to do our work."

"Yeah, well, maybe I have a life beyond the family."

Her chest heaved with the frustration she felt. "Maybe I've got things to do."

Corey stood straighter and looked down his nose at her. "There is no life beyond the family. There is nothing you need to do but be part of us. There is nothing greater."

How Debra hated his superior tone. Anger ran rampant in her, and she couldn't, wouldn't look at Mother. She turned to leave, but a sudden voice in her head whirled her around. She swung her large, very heavy computer bag at Corey, striking him in the left temple. Instantly blood poured from the side of his shocked face and he went down. Debra watched him twitch, smearing his own blood pooling on the pooled on the worn wooden floor.

"Nice." Debra said under her breath. "Now, all is well."

She got a brief glimpse of Mother's anguished expression, and she laughed as she left through the back door.

Once in her car, Debra laid her forehead on the steering wheel, clutching her hands together in her lap. It was over. She was no longer part of the beautiful Benevolent Angels, doing God's work by bringing peace to the elderly,

"What about my goddamned peace?" she said loudly, as she sat back and switched on the ignition. "Don't I deserve a little peace?"

Sudden grief filled her, as she thought of all she'd lost. The family had loved her once, more so than her own birth mother ever did. She had found a type of peace with them. Then Mol—

Debra pushed these thoughts away, as she headed toward town. It was almost dusk and the lights of

Queens Lot seemed welcoming. Ten minutes later, she pulled into her driveway and noted that there were no lights to welcome her. She'd left the gate open that morning, and she wondered idly if the dogs had found new homes. She'd removed their collars a couple days ago, and she hoped that Maryann Findlay, the dog lover down the road a short piece, would understand that she could keep them.

Debra entered the darkened house and felt her way into the kitchen. She opened the refrigerator, and her mother's skull and face winked at her from the depths before vanishing into the cold, thin air.

"Hey, Mama." Debra whispered. "I let the dogs loose. I know it's probably not what you wanted but, believe you me, it's better for them. I'm not exactly hitting on all thrusters right about now, am I?"

She reached past the wilted lettuce and a moldy green pepper, and brought out a cold brew. She let the fridge slide shut and walked carefully into the darkened living room. She sat in Mol's chair and thoughtfully sipped her beer. *This is nice,* she thought. *This is good.*

Chapter Thirty-five

"YOU'VE GOT TO COME back, Lacey. Wade is here, taking over, and he's undoing everything you've put in place since you became Sheriff.

Lacey leaned her head back against the sofa and shifted Ben, who was happily dozing in her lap. "I'm allowed bereavement leave, Erva. It's in my contract."

"Yeah, well, Wade just don't care about that. He sees it as his chance just to move right in and make hisself to home."

"Fucking prick." Lacey sighed loudly. These ten days of peace had been sorely needed after her grandmother's death, but she supposed it was time to take on life again. She needed to get back on duty and find the bastard who killed her grandmother.

"Amen to that. Listen, he stopped all investigation into the murders. Says it's hogwash and that you're just trying to drum up business. I swear to God, that's what he said."

"Fucking prick. All right. Listen, it's late in the day, so I'll just be in tomorrow morning, bright and early. Don't let him do too much damage between now and then, okay?"

"Yeah. Like stopping a steam roller though. I don't know why he thinks he's so much better at being Sheriff than you are. All he does is sit around and bullshit with his friends who drop by."

"It's 'cause he has a penis and I don't. Makes him more special."

"Fucking prick," Erva agreed.

After Erva signed off, Lacey pulled Ben up and showered kisses all over his white and black Siamese face. He protested loudly, and when she set him aside, he shook and groomed as though she'd made him horribly dirty. He looked at her with reproach in his bright-blue, slightly crossed eyes.

"Yeah, yeah, get over it," Lacey chided, rising and heading into the kitchen for another cup of iced coffee.

She had enjoyed these days off work. They had given her time to think about her life and the direction she was heading in. They also gave her time to think about her new, immense attraction to Sloane Stevens. After their evening together, a text message had popped up on her phone the next day, the day before the funeral. Sloane said she'd gotten the number from Erva and hoped that Lacey didn't mind. Lacey had assured her in the biggest way that not only didn't she mind, but here was her email and messaging information. This had led to a steady back and forth conversation in long, rambling emails, quick thinking-of-your texts, as well as breathy late-night phone calls.

Oh, they had been the souls of decorum at the funeral, Lacey up front with the family and Sloane in the general pews. The funeral was well attended and an exhausted Lacey looked around after it was over only to find that Sloane had left after offering condolences to the Terry family. Bertie was there, though, and this created a whole new set of problems. Lacey really wanted to share these new feelings with Bertie, whom she considered a friend, but was afraid of the feelings of abandonment this might spawn in Bertie. Or maybe rejection?

She and Bertie had been afraid of coming out in Queens Lot, but here was Lacey, really ready to head into an open lesbian relationship with no tangible qualms. She was refusing to let the townsfolk dictate how she lived. Not anymore. Life was just too, too short for that nonsense. Her beloved Nanna's death had proven that. Lacey sometimes imagined she heard her Nanna's voice, assuring her that she'd made the right decision. This still didn't help with the Bertie situation, but she knew that she couldn't let Bertie make decisions for her either. She would have a good, candid talk with Bertie. Maybe she would surprise Lacey and take it as well as her mother had.

While working with her mom to get Nanna's things out of her house so they could sell it, Lacey had broached the subject. The conversation would stay with her forever.

"Hey, Mom. What would you and Dad do if I...uh...if I wanted to date...uh...date a woman?"

She closed her eyes, waiting for the haranguing to begin, but her mother answered quietly, absently, as she continued to sort through papers. "Well, I'm sure we'd say who is she? Is she nice? Is she good to you?"

Lacey was baffled by the response. "But. But you wouldn't be upset?"
Her mother finally looked at her, patiently laying aside the paperwork. "You mean that you're a lesbian? Of course not. We've known that since you were twelve and had a crush on Lucy Phillips. Remember how you used to hold hands and make up songs about Lacey and Lucy and how lucky you were?"

"Oh. My. God," Lacey groaned, dropping her head in her hands. "You've known since then?"

"Well, sure. Your dad and I talked about it a long time, finally concluding we didn't care about your sexual orientation, as long as you were happy. We do want grandchildren though, so just be cognizant of that, okay?"

"Why didn't you say something?"

Joy shook her head in the negative. "Not our place, hon. We just let you have your space to follow your heart."

"But all those guys Erva tried to set me up with, that you tried to set me up with..."

"You're missing the point, Lacey. We don't care what gender you date, male or female. That's up to you. We just introduce you to nice people, the rest is up to you. Unfortunately, we don't know any other lesbians, or we would have introduced you to them."

Lacey laughed uncontrollably at that point, from relief as much as from joy. And when her mother asked who Lacey was interested in, because obviously, she would have never brought it up otherwise, Lacey gushed on and on about Sloane.

Remembering this, Lacey had to smile, but the smile faded when her cell rang. It was Bertie and she sounded harried.

"Hey, Lacey. Do you know Frank just pulled me over on the way home?"

"No, I didn't. What was it? Were you speeding?"

"Hell, no. He wanted to sell me tickets on a truck raffle. Pulled me over to sell me tickets for a truck! Can you even believe it?"

Lacey had to chuckle. "It's Wade. He's back in

charge, while I've been out on bereavement."

"Oh, you're kidding me."

"Nope, serious as a heart attack. Erva just called and begged me to come back, so I'm going in tomorrow."

"Good. That's a good thing. How are you holding up?"

Lacey could hear the warm concern grow in Bertie's voice, and guilt marched through her with big feet. "Oh, I'm okay. I miss her. A lot, but I'll just have to come to grips with it. Listen, Bertie. I was wondering if you could meet me for lunch tomorrow? I'll come by the school with something from the Thai place. There's something we need to discuss, and I don't really want to do it over the phone.

"Sure, okay," Bertie said, voice confused. "Twelve thirty would be good."

Lacey signed off and looked at Ben, who had curled into a silent ball of snuggly in a back corner of the sofa.

Chapter Thirty-six

WADE WAS ALREADY THERE when Lacey walked in the next morning. He was sitting in her office. Sitting in her chair. Fury leapt up in her, but she managed to maintain her cool.

"Hello, Wade. Can't thank you enough for stepping in to cover for me."

She stood at her desk, obviously waiting for him to move. Even his smarmy presence couldn't take away the good mood that had been fostered by an early morning phone conversation with Sloane.

Wade stood and hitched up his jeans. He'd put on a bit of weight since the election, and Lacey was not surprised that he wasn't in uniform. It probably would be too tight at this point.

"Hello, Lacey. Welcome back. So sad about your grandma, but you know she'd want you to muddle on."

Muddle on? Lacey just smiled politely, as she stepped past him to regain her seat as Sheriff. "Anything I need to know about?"

He shook his head, and Lacey realized, by looking into his haunted eyes, that this job had been his life. A divorced father of two grown sons, he had nothing else. Compassion swelled in her, and she made a firm resolution to find some type of volunteer work for him in the department. Truthfully, he was no different, certainly no worse, than some of the other people in town. His good-old-boy network might just be of some value to the office.

"I really do appreciate your help, Wade. You're a good man."

Wade, who'd made it to the door, suddenly turned back. "Oh, one thing. Frank done brought in a crazy during the night. Locked her up 'til we can get her over to the med center for an evaluation."

"A crazy? What—?" Lacey realized she was talking to thin air. She looked at the desktop and straightened a few things then sought out Erva.

"So, what's this about a crazy?"

Erva looked up from the financial ledger. "Oh, my gawd, Lacey you won't even believe. Frank was on duty last night and took a little patrol around town, just after midnight. What does he find but a naked woman just taking her time, strolling down Central Avenue."

Lacey couldn't help the grin that crawled across her face. "No shit? Really?"

Erva was grinning, too. "Really. She looks familiar to me, but I can't place her. Maybe you'll have better luck."

She rose and Lacey walked with her to the long back corridor where the holding cells were. They heard the woman muttering as soon as they entered the hallway. Erva led the way to the first cell on the left.

Peering in, Lacey gasped. "Well, I believe that's Debra...something. She works over at King's. Manager, if I remember correctly."

Erva poked at her bottom lip with a thumbnail. "Ah, that's where I've seen her. Thought she looked familiar."

Lacey studied the rapidly pacing woman. She was

disheveled, her short blonde curls unbrushed and her round face flushed. She was wearing a Coves County coverall, but she had unbuttoned it so the white skin of her upper body shone through. County provided slippers flopped on her feet as she paced.

"Debra? How we doing today? You feeling all right?" Lacey asked gently, as she moved closer to the cell.

Abruptly, Debra rushed at the bars, causing Lacey to step back in fear.

"I can do it, goddamn it, I can!" she shouted.

Lacey kept her voice calm, though she was alarmed at the crazy glowing bright in Debra's bloodshot eyes. "Sure, sure you can Debra. What is it you can do?"

"Just because I was late taking Nancy's money don't mean nothing. There's plenty of other beloveds to take. Lots of old people in this stupid town."

She turned away abruptly and began her rapid pacing, talking loudly to herself. "Corey needed to die, too, arrogant bastard. I hope he fuckin' bleeds to death." Her voice changed to a plaintive wail. "Oh, Mother, Mother, love me, please. Love me like you used to, Mother."

Lacey looked at Erva, and Erva looked back, eyes wide.

"What the hell?" Erva whispered. "You think she killed somebody?"

"Hell, maybe she's the somebody who killed lots of people here in the Lot," Lacey responded.

"Hey, Debra, who's Corey?" Lacey asked the woman in the cell.

Debra stopped pacing and looked at Lacey. "You know, I couldn't tell Mother about Mama. I didn't kill her the right way, and Mother told us a long time ago that it was unforgivable. Respect is the second commandment, second only to choose wisely. She taught us this while we were still in the trances."

A very bad feeling began to bloom in the pit of Lacey's stomach. This was seriously beyond just a crazy woman scattering her marbles. Frankly, what Debra was saying was beginning to terrify her.

Debra finally stopped pacing, and she curled her full figure into a ball on the cot. She stuck her thumb between her teeth. The silence was enormous when she quieted.

"Erva, I got a bad feeling about this. Let's get Jimmy over here to stay with her and write down everything she says. Just put a chair here and give him a pad. I'm gonna get Sully and check out her house, see what we can see."

Chapter Thirty-seven

ACCORDING TO THE 911 map, Mol Allison owned a house just south of town on one of the secondary roads off Grey Street.

"You don't think that crazy woman could have actually killed anyone, do you?" Sully asked, as they turned into the driveway.

"I don't know," Lacey responded, "but it sure feels weird. I mean, all that stuff she's saying...I just don't know what to think."

The wood-framed, clapboard house was in bad shape. It could have used some paint and also some clutter control. There were broken lawn chairs, wooden crates, and cracked planters crowding the base of the home. There was a broken down wooden fence an open wooden gate hanging askew. A dark-green Ford Taurus sat in the driveway, the driver's door yawning wide.

"This place is a dump," Sully said, as they left the cruiser and stood by the front door.

"Shh, the woman will hear you," Lacey chided. There was no doorbell, so she knocked forcefully on the door. To her surprise, the barely latched door fell open.

Lacey looked at Sully, and then nodded toward the door, indicating that he should go first. Sully drew his gun and clicked off the safety. He pushed the door open and stepped inside. Lacey followed.

"Miss Allison? It's Sheriff Terry. We're coming in."

There was no answer, and the two stood in the center of the cluttered front room of the house. The first thing that drew their eyes was the writing on the far-right wall. Someone had scrawled *Bitch dog mother* across the fleur-de-lis wallpaper in what looked like red lipstick.

"Whoa," Sully exclaimed quietly.

Dark-brown beer bottles and food wrappers were heaped in about five or six different piles across the living room floor. The only clear path was the few feet between a tattered easy chair and an older model television. Lacey kicked aside a Hardee's bag and moved toward the kitchen.

"Shit!" she said.

The kitchen was just as trashed as the living room and filled with the odor of rotting garbage. Lacey saw dog paw prints in some of the filth on the floor but didn't see or hear any dogs. The waste bin was overflowing, and a few flies had hatched out of somewhere and were buzzing lazily about the mess. The counters were spread with two cutting boards and knives smeared with a dark, viscous liquid. The sink overflowed with dirty dishes, and cockroaches scattered as Lacey approached. She noted that someone had left what looked like chunks of bloody ham to just rot in the sink

"Oh, good Christ," Sully said behind her.

Lacey just shook her head and brushed past him into the hall leading toward the back of the house. She passed a small bathroom and paused to peer in. There was more disarray in there. Someone had drawn houses and smiling people across the mirror with blue-striped toothpaste. Lacey pushed the shower curtain aside but found nothing but shampoo bottles behind it.

Farther along the hallway, she found a clothes-cluttered laundry room and then another bedroom, notable for its abundance of deadbolts that ran along the door's edge.

"Wonder why she was locking the door," Sully mused behind her.

Lacey shrugged and pushed the door open. The small bedroom was neat, especially compared to the rest of the house. Three long tables lined the room. All had computers or other electronic equipment on top. Two of the monitors had been imploded with a hammer, which still lay on the table next to one.

"Mind the glass," Lacey muttered, as she moved past the tables and around the double bed. She opened the closet next to the bed and saw Debra's pale-blue work smocks, her name neatly embroidered on the front left placket.

"This must be Debra's room," Lacey said. "Guess the computers were hers."

"Why so many, though? Seems weird." Sully was frowning at the machines.

"Everything about this is weird," Lacey responded.

Something on the bed pillows caught her eyes, and she leaned closer to get a better look. She sprang back almost immediately, knocking into Sully and almost toppling one of the tables.

"What? What happened?" Sully asked, trying to see around Lacey.

"The bed...it's..."

"What is it?" Sully strained to see.

"It's a...hand. A hand." Lacey whispered, feeling nausea well. She forced herself to look again and yes, it was a mummified, shriveled hand, probably a woman's, with long, yellowed fingernails. It had been placed with care atop one of the two pillows.

Lacey turned away and pushed past Sully.

"Don't touch it," she warned unnecessarily, as she fished her radio from her belt.

She pressed the call button. "Erva, come in. Hey, Erva! You there?"

Impatient seconds passed until Erva answered. "Hey, Sheriff, I'm here. Over."

"We got a crime scene. Can you call the county forensic team and get them out here? Mol's address. Over."

"Will do, Sheriff. Hey, that woman was talking again, and Jimmy's been taking down everything. Have you ever heard of a place in town called the Lawrence house? Over."

Lacey mulled the name a few seconds. "Yeah, isn't that the place where that old lady, Rebecca Lawrence, lived? Outside town? Over."

"Oh, right. She went into the nursing home, didn't she? Who bought the house? Over."

Sudden static caused Lacey to move the radio farther from her face. "Good question," she said when the static died down. "Can you check on that for me? Over."

"Sure, will do. Over."

Lacey had moved along the hallway while talking to Erva. She was trying to force the image of the hand from her mind, and she opened the next door she came to with some trepidation. Her fear was unwarranted for the room was just another, larger bedroom. It was cluttered with various piles of shopping bags and strange possessions that looked like thrift store discards. No bodies though, and Lacey sighed with relief. She looked into the large, mirrored closet and saw a wealth of outdated dresses and shoes. She checked in the stacked cardboard boxes but found only mementos and photos of Mol and some children that Lacey didn't know, although one looked a little like Debra. She closed the closet and moved into the bathroom.

A large, beige acrylic tub was the biggest feature of this mostly nondescript room. As Lacey moved closer, she could see that the separation joints where tub met the inset acrylic wall covering were crusted with rusty brown. Could that be rust? Or blood? Dried blood?

The cabinet under the sink had popped open. Lacey pulled the cabinet all the way open and a pile of blood-stiffened towels toppled out. They had been folded and perfectly stacked, probably while freshly saturated, but they had dried into a crusty, hard cache that had forced the door open as they dried.

"Ugh!" Sully said, looking over her shoulder.

"You got that right," Lacey said, wrinkling her nose. "What the hell happened in this house?"

Sudden reggae music played from Lacey's phone, and she quickly silenced it.

"Hey, Erva. What did you find out?"

"It's owned by someone named Corey Tallmayer. Never heard of him, have you?"

Lacey shook her head. "No, never have. Might be an out of towner. Does he live there or is it a summer house?"

"Says primary residence, so I'm thinking he lives there. Bought it almost four years ago."

"Hey," Lacey paused. "Didn't Debra say something about a Corey?"

"Yeah." She rattled papers. "A couple times. He

might be dead, looks like."

Lacey rubbed her forehead with the finger pads of her free hand. "God's knees. This is just crazy."

"So, what are you gonna do, Lacey?" Erva's voice rang with concern.

"Well, I'm going out there. Listen, I'm leaving Sully here to mind the crime scene, but I'll run over to the Lawrence house and see what I can see. If I remember correctly, it's not far from here."

"You be careful, Lacey," Erva warned. "You have no idea what you'll be walking into out there."

"Yeah, I know. Hey, why don't you rustle Frank out of bed and send him to the Lawrence house, too, for backup. Just in case. Tell him to hurry up."

"Will do. Call me if you need anything." Erva was clearly worried.

So was Lacey.

Chapter Thirty-eight

THE DRIVEWAY TO THE Lawrence property was a ldirt road, almost a mile long. Lacey rolled down it slowly, wondering what she would encounter. Maybe Debra was just talking out of her head, and Lacey was on her way to interrupting someone's daily life. She fervently hoped that was the case. The idea that someone was killing elderly people in the Lot was bad enough, but to think that Debra had killed the owner of the Lawrence property in some kind of serial killer plot between the two of them was a little horrifying. Especially in quiet little Queens Lot.

The house came into view and it looked deserted. Obviously, the new owner hadn't wanted to do a lot of work on the place.

Lacey pressed her foot on the brake and rolled into the cleared area in front of the house as quietly as possible. She let down her window and listened. She heard nothing but late season crickets singing to one another. She stepped from the car and decided to scout out the territory before approaching the front door. She walked around the side but paused when she heard voices.

"We just need to pack up and go," a woman, said.

"She's going to cause all kinds of trouble. Suppose she talks about us," a man said.

"I'll miss him so much," said a woman with a high-pitched, girlish voice. "He was my friend."

There were several unintelligible exchanges, so Lacey moved close to one of the windows and peered in. A young woman with long, blond hair was close to the window. She was turned away and seemed to be dragging a large trunk behind her. A difficult task since one arm was twisted by scars and seemed useless.

Lacey gasped, as a sudden memory surfaced. What had her mother said during that dinner that seemed so long ago?

"She's having dinner with a new friend. It's this young woman she met at King's. Someone new to town...Her name is Sarah, and Mama says that she is just the most pitiful thing. She's been in a house fire, and she has scars all over her arms and face."

Lacey ducked and turned back to the window, hoping she hadn't been heard. Had this woman killed her grandmother?

Anger grew in her, as she watched a handsome young man with long, dark hair come and help the burned woman with the trunk. He looked just like the sketch Frances had made based on Alexa Hales' description. Had these two been murdering people in her town?

Filled with fury, Lacey drew her gun from its holster and walked forward and peered around the corner. She made sure no one was there then moved across the wide back of the house, glad for the huge sweet gum tree that gave her some shadow. A trio of cars was parked out back, but sound from the screen door squeaking open drew her attention away from examining them.

A tall, skinny blond man came down the back steps, a stuffed garbage bag in his hands. Without even thinking, Lacey moved quickly behind him and slammed her gun into the back of his skull. He went down with only a muffled groan. Lacey turned his limp body until she found his hands. She snapped her cuffs loose from her belt and slid them on his wrists.

Panting, she pulled his unconscious form closer to the house, out of direct sight of the doorway. She crouched there, trying to decide her next move. Precious minutes ticked by as she dealt with her indecision. There was no more activity near the back door, so she crept closer, trying to keep her feet from rustling in the crunchy fall leaves underfoot.

She paused at the closest side of the three wooden steps coming from the back door and listened. She flattened against the house just as steps sounded and the screen door swung open. A woman descended, a very thin woman with a shaved head and dark skin. She was humming a song and struggling to carry a well-filled, army-green backpack. She got to the bottom of the steps before she saw Lacey, and when she did, her dull, jaundiced eyes grew very large. Lacey brought a finger to her lips in the universal sign for quiet. Surprising her, the woman threw the backpack toward her and took off running through the scrub brush, heading east, away from the house.

Lacey sighed and took mental note of the woman's direction. She was just glad she hadn't screamed, thereby giving away Lacey's element of surprise. Lacey rolled the backpack away from her feet and listened intently. She heard the faint, irregular tinkle of glass, but that was the only sound. Stealthily, heart beating too loud in her chest, Lacey mounted the steps and, ever so slowly, opened the door.

Chapter Thirty-nine

THE ROOM SHE STEPPED into was deserted. It was a kitchen, with surprisingly modern in appliances and dining furniture and a clean, vinyl tiled floor. A large cardboard box rested on the table, jarring in the room's neatness. Peering in, Lacey saw that it was filled with canned and boxed food. Obviously, the murderers were packing for a move, evidenced by the wide-open, empty cabinets. Anger sparked anew in Lacey. How dare they think they could get away?

She crept forward, toward the sound of glassware being moved. She stayed very close to the wall so her careful footsteps wouldn't make the floorboards creak. She peeped around the door jamb and saw, across the hall, the burned girl and the dark-haired boy packing up what looked like a laboratory filled with various bottles of colored liquid, pale beige and pink mostly. They were putting stoppers in the bottles and placing them carefully into the trunk. The boy moved to some piping strung above the lab tables and began to dismantle it.

"Hello, Lacey. I wondered when you would come," said a very familiar voice.

Lacey closed her eyes in a moment of sheer agony, before she turned and faced the woman who'd spoken. It was her Bertie, but it wasn't her Bertie. This woman had long, dark hair and was wearing ripped jeans and a Rolling Stones T-shirt. She wore black leather combat boots on her feet, but they had been left mostly untied and gaped open in the front. Gone was the conservative school teacher with her sensible clothing.

Lacey had a momentary reprieve thinking that this had to be a twin. An evil twin, one who was like night and day with her Bertie. But the woman leaned forward and swung off the wig. Indeed, it was her Bertie with short, thick, blond hair.

"I guess this comes as something of a shock." Bertie tossed the wig to one side and ruffled her fingers through her real hair. The wig landed on an overstuffed sofa, but the weight of it caused it to slither down the side and onto the floor as though it were a live animal.

Lacey found her voice and it was fueled by anger. "Did you kill my people, Bertie? Are you the one who listened to me go on and on about..." She paused and shook her head from side to side. "How could you do this, Bertie? This is not..."

"What? Me? Of course, it is." She waved away Lacey's words. "You just never took the time to know the real me."

"Oh no, no, no! Don't you dare try to put any of this on me. I trusted you, Bertie. You were my friend, you were my...my lover." Her voice dropped, and a sob somehow found its way out.

"You don't understand, Lacey. This is our mission in life, our mission from God. We take away the pain and suffering that inevitably infect our beloved, the elderly who live among us."

"You killed my grandmother, you bitch!" Lacey cried out. She lifted her weapon and pointed it at Bertie. "She was not in pain, she was not suffering. You had no right, no matter what grand mission you say you follow."

"Now would be a good time, Angel," Bertie said.

It felt like a bee stung Lacey in the neck. She spun and saw the burned girl was holding a small syringe in her good hand. The world went dark.

Chapter Forty

LACEY'S HEAD WAS POUNDING, and her mouth was as dry as a cotton boll in high summer. She moved her tongue up and down to try and moisten the cavern of her mouth, but it was useless. The harsh chemical taste in her mouth made her feel sick. She fought retching, mostly because her head hurt too much.

"It's just the date-rape part, not the poison," Bertie said in a low voice. "I understand it's pretty brutal. The poison, of course, would be lethal. Sarah really is a chemical mastermind. The concoctions she comes up with..."

Lacey carefully turned her head in Bertie's direction. "Tastes like shit," she rasped out.

Her eyes swept to one side, just beyond Bertie. She saw the burned girl and the dark-haired boy lying supine, side by side, on the hard, wooden floor. Their hands were crossed over their chests, and it was easy to see that they were both dead.

Bertie noted her interest. "I had to take them. Sarah didn't choose wisely, and Danny can't go because I have to re-establish, yet again. One more fucking time..." She looked at Lacey. "You know, I almost took you, too. I know I should have, but I just had to wait and tell you that Sarah taking your grandmother was a mistake. It was too close to home for us. When I found out, I knew everything here in Queens Lot was over." She sighed as if the weight of the world was on her shoulders.

Lacey sat up straighter in the chair she was in and realized that she was bound to that wooden chair by a variety of bindings, a belt on one arm, a scarf on the other, and ropes on both her feet.

"What the fuck? Let me go." Lacey twisted but the binds were too tight. In fact, her fingers were tingling from the tightness, the circulation compromised

Bertie shook her head and lifted her dark, haunted eyes to Lacey. "Can't let you go, hon. Gotta clean up after myself."

Lacey stopped squirming as new information filtered into her brain. "You don't even use your real name, do you? Who are you?"

"I'm who I need to be, Lacey."

Lacey watched her keenly, trying to unravel the puzzle that was Bertie. "How do you murder people? With no apology. What you just said wasn't even an apology. How do you get these others to murder people? You take human life, for God's sake!"

Bertie stood and looked at the two bodies on the floor. "Yes, for God's sake. We end suffering. We end aging and hardship. We call ourselves the Benevolent Angels, and I am their mother. I care for them, they care for me, and we all do God's will."

"How long?" Lacey said, trying to swallow.

"How long have we been doing this? Forever."

Bertie lit a cigarette and walked to a chest sitting on the coffee table, smoke trailing behind her. The chest was small, inlaid with gold leaf and decorated with beautiful, rich tapestry. "They're all here," she said, running her fingers lovingly across the top.

"They? They who?" Lacey wished her hands were free just so she could hold her aching head. "Are those ashes of the people you've killed?"

Bertie grimaced at her. "Of course not. It's their lights, their beautiful lights."

"Look, Bertie, or whatever your name is. This has to stop. You can't continue to kill people. It doesn't matter if they're old or ready to die anyway. It has to stop."

"I wish it could," Bertie whispered. "You have to realize that I have no choice in the matter. I was born with a gift that allows me to see what others can't see. This gift allows me to know God's will and enables me to do that will."

"Yada, yada," Lacey said sarcastically. She'd had enough of this idiocy. She fought her bindings again, but again, to no avail.

Suddenly, Bertie threw her cigarette into a bucket next to the sofa and immediate flame billowed from it. A harsh, acrid odor filled the air. Then Bertie was in front of her. Very close. Lacey stilled and lifted her gaze. Bertie's hand shot out and grasped her jaw roughly, her fingers bending and digging fingernails into the soft skin of Lacey's face.

"You people," she hissed. "You never understand the beauty of what I do." She linked their gazes, and a strange sensation rose in Lacey. She fought it but the pain in her face somehow riveted her, and she felt an overwhelming, physical compulsion to kiss Bertie. She also felt childlike, her own free will crumbling. She very badly wanted to please Bertie, to make her proud.

A stealthy sound outside drew Bertie's gaze away from her, and Lacey whimpered with a sudden ache of loss. Bertie ran to the window then lifted the case of 'lights' and moved back to Lacey.

"They've found us, my sweet angel," she said, stroking Lacey's cheek lovingly. "I'm sorry, there's no time for me to give you the gift of eternity. There's just no time."

Bertie stepped away and looked back once, as she headed toward the kitchen and back door. "I would have stayed with you. If I could have. I want you to know that."

As soon as she was out of sight, the hypnotic trance spawned by Bertie dissipated. She shook her head and worked her jaw from side to side. She began yelling loudly, so Frank would come rescue her. Within seconds, the front door imploded, but it was Sully, not Frank. He glanced once at the two bodies, then at the fire before rushing to untie Lacey.

"Frank stayed at the Allison house," he muttered absently, as his fingers plucked at her bindings.

Stinking smoke was filling the room, as the sofa caught fire and blazed toward the curtains and a nearby chair. Sully's eyes were soon weeping from the smoke, and Lacey's throat began to close.

"She must have used an accelerant," Lacey choked out.

Sully nodded, but was having no luck with the knots, although he'd managed to unbuckle the belt.

Lacey wriggled her hand free from the belt and used that hand to tug at the scarf, while Sully fished out his pocketknife and used it on the ropes at her feet. Within seconds, she was free but it wasn't a moment too soon. Hot flames chased them out the back door of the house, and they both rolled on the leafy ground outside, coughing, trying to get their lungs to resume working.

"Fuck, where'd she go?" Lacey said, when she could.

"I dunno," Sully said, swiping at his face. "Was she still in there? Sounded like it." He coughed loudly.

Lacey watched the old house burn like a matchhead. "She had this planned," she muttered, then coughed once more to remove any lingering smoke. She stood, unsteadily, and swiveled her head. "Did you get the blond boy?"

Sully looked at her blankly and shook his head in the negative as he coughed again. "Didn't see no boy," he rasped out.

She searched the entire yard behind the house and both sides. The young man and the green backpack were missing. She noted one of the cars was missing but had no idea which one it was and what it looked like.

Chapter Forty-one

"I BET THAT BERTIE woman killed the new owner of the Lawrence house and took it over, don't you?" Sully asked. "Otherwise, he woulda told someone. Wonder where his body is?"

Sully, Erva, and Lacey were at the break room table, having coffee at the sheriff's department. He lifted his cup and took a hefty swallow.

"Still can't believe it happened," Erva said, leaning lazily on one arm as she sipped from her cup.

"Well, according to the powers that be, it didn't," Lacey added bitterly.

No policeman but Sully, who had heard some of the exchange, believed that serial killers had been at work in Queens Lot. The official record from the Coves County forensic team was that Debra had killed her mother and was now insane from the guilt and grief she harbored. Her words and wild claims could not be proven. The murder of Mol Allison and the aftermath had provided weeks of gossip for the small community, however.

This continued disbelief from those in authority sickened and angered Lacey, but there was nothing she could do about it. She had absolutely no proof to corroborate her and Sully's account of that day. Even the charred bodies gave up no clues as their dental records were not in any local or national database. Clevon told her that news with an offensive 'told you so' look in his eyes. His final report said that they were probably squatters, druggies caught up in a house fire, no doubt caused by the meth lab they'd set up there. The owner of the property had never been located, so what remained of the house and the land that it stood on would eventually revert back to the county.

"So, Sloane," Erva said teasingly. "Never woulda thought it."

Sully grunted and rose to leave, as he always did when Lacey's now very open private life was mentioned.

Lacey grinned at Erva and nodded her head toward Sully's retreating back. She somehow found much humor in the small amount of confused shunning she had received from the townsfolk. Compared to the Allison murder, her dating Sloane was definitely small potatoes.

At least Sloane seemed to believe Lacey's story, but it was probably because she trusted and cared for Lacey. Erva also believed her word, as did her parents, and this faith from those closest to her brought her back to full autonomy and faith in herself. Sloane had been a true anchor for Lacey during the past few weeks, as Lacey sorted through a number of uncomfortable feelings.

Lacey briefly thought about giving up her post. She'd been really unnerved by the murders but she decided to remain as Sheriff of Queens Lot. The murders and nature of the perpetrators had changed her outlook, however. She would never be as trusting

and open as before. She would also never stop looking for the woman who had caused her beloved, beautiful grandmother to die before her time.

It was frustrating though. Sending out an APB on Bertie would have been useless, because she was like a chameleon. Lacey was sure, with no doubt, that Bertie looked different already. Lacey had no idea who the blond boy was or where he'd come from. No one had reported any young man missing from the Lot.

"Yeah," Lacey agreed with Erva. "I never would have either. She's pretty amazing though." She tossed her empty cup into the bin for two points. "I'm thinking about asking her to move in."

Erva reached across the table and took Lacey's hand. She leaned her upper body on the table and stared up at Lacey so their eyes could meet. "I think that's an excellent idea."

Back in her office, Lacey thought back through her time with Bertie, even their intimate times together. She realized right away that there had been no real clue that she was up to something. No indication that she had another family, made up of serial killers. There were some unexplained absences and a school teacher's penchant for the young, but not much else.

Lacey pulled over yet another huge mug-shot book and began turning pages. She did this a lot these days, looking for a familiar face.

Her one hope was that the skinny black woman would be spotted among the homeless of the town. After work, she often moseyed down to the rail yard, looking around but telling herself it was because she wanted a coffee from Ellen's coffee shop. She would sit there and drink warm lattes, remembering the times she and Bertie had shared the stories of their lives over morning or afternoon coffee. Now, she wondered how many of those stories that Bertie shared were true.

Probably none.

The End
Or the Beginning?

About Nat Burns

Nat Burns retired from a medical publishing career and became a full-time novelist in 2007. Since then she has published thirteen novels with four different publishers. Two more are under contract for release in early 2018.

During ten years as a journalist, Burns won two Virginia Press Association awards, as well as honors from Writer's Digest, Writers in Virginia, The Virginia Writing Club, Piedmont Writing Institute and Writers of the Future. She taught journalism and creative writing as part of the Writers in Virginia program and worked with the Small Press Writer and Artist Organization for many years, serving one year as president. She has written a monthly column called "Notes from Nat" with a magazine in Los Angeles for more than ten years.

Since becoming a novelist, Burns won one Golden Crown Literary Award and twice was voted a finalist. She also won the 2011 Alice B. Lavender Certificate for her novel *Two Weeks in August*. Her poem, "Womanwalk", won first place in a local Virginia Writing Club contest and third place in the state competition.

As an editor, Burns worked with VA NOW, Byrd Newspapers, County of Nelson, Hampton Roads Publishing and Carden Jennings Publishing. She has edited more than three dozen fiction and non-fiction books, many of them winning awards.

Complete information can be found at natburns.org or natburns.com

Note to Readers:

Thank you for reading a book from Desert Palm Press. We have made every effort to edit this book. However, typos do slip in. If you find an error in the text, please email lee@desertpalmpress.com so the issue can be corrected.

We appreciate you as a reader and want to ensure you enjoy the reading process. We would like you to consider posting a review on your preferred media sites such as Amazon, Smashwords, Bella Books, Goodreads, Tumblr, Twitter, Facebook, and/or your blog or website.

For more information on upcoming releases, author interviews, contest, giveaways and more, please sign up for our newsletter and visit us as at Desert Palm Press: www.desertpalmpress.com and "Like" us on Facebook: Desert Palm Press.

Bright Blessings